MW00780284

Submerged

Chloe Briggs

Submerged © 2024 Chloe Briggs

All Rights Reserved

ISBN: 979-8-9908409-0-4 (paperback)

This is a work of fiction.

The characters in this novel are entirely fictional and are products of the author's imagination.

Any resemblance to actual persons living or dead is entirely coincidental.

The day I said, "I do," I thought we reached perfection.

Little did I know it was the calm before the storm.

- Emily

iv

Chapter 1

In the Beginning

EMILY

I was abruptly awakened by the sensation of someone staring at me. I opened my eyes and was startled by my mother standing over me. Her eyes, glassy and black, as though she were staring into an abyss of nothingness. Her demeanor of confusion rattled me to my core. She was unkempt and her clothes were dirty from the day prior.

"Who are you and who sent you here? Did Satan send you?"

"No mama, it's me, Emily." I was rattled and scared. Barely awake. I felt like I was dreaming. "I'm your daughter."

I had just turned eight years old.

"Lies!!!! The devil tells lies. I don't have a daughter. Get thee behind me Satan!"

I was terrified. My dad worked the third shift, and he wouldn't be home for hours. She turned her back from me and I jumped from the other side of the bed and ran. I ran out the back door and into the field behind our home. I had a fort that I built with my best friend who lived across the street. I found refuge there.

I could hear her screaming from the house calling for Satan. *No mama, it's just me, Emily. I'm cold and scared mama. Why are you doing this? I love you.*

Tears flowed from my eyes, and I curled into a ball in the fluffiest part of the field. It was a chilled evening, and I could hear the frogs in the nearby creak. The air smelled damp and of early morning dew. Thank God I wore my footed pajamas to bed. I rocked and rocked until I fell asleep. It would be hours until my dad found me.

It was the beginning of an abominable childhood. To say I was traumatized is an understatement.

I was an only child to Andrew and Angela Brooks. We lived in a small rural town in Ohio. The one in which everyone knew each other. One grocery store, one gas station, one bank, one pharmacy and one drive thru liquor store. There was a total of two traffic lights in our micro town and we had just what we needed to get by. I wanted to escape my life and I knew I had the potential to. I knew I was smart. I spent a good portion of my childhood reading. The stories I would read took me to unimaginable places and I felt like I was experiencing adventures. Often, I was alone, and reading was my only comfort. My love of reading helped me to embrace my passion for writing. I always had a vivid and creative imagination. I would create worlds that would whisk me away and I would fantasize about another place and time. A place where I could be whatever I wanted to be, and I could take away the pain from those I loved. I could take away my pain. As a child, I remember sitting in my elementary classroom, staring out the window as the fall leaves fell briskly to the ground from the autumn winds. Swirls of orange, golden-yellow, and green filled the air. The classroom smelled of burnt dust from the furnace kicking on. I could hear the girls in class as they giggled and laughed about plans, they had made for their weekend sleepovers and birthday parties.

Submerged

My mother was schizophrenic, and she enjoyed her alcohol. We later found out that the alcohol masked the disease. She mostly drank at night once I was in bed, but this led to many mornings of me getting ready for school on my own. When her disease was under control, that's when I caught glimpses of my young and vibrant mom, and that's when she was one of my favorite people. She was one of the prettiest moms in the neighborhood and she took such good care of our home and yard. She often wore her auburn hair down like Farrah Fawcett and she had a very petite figure. I can recall hot summer days when the sun was at its peak. My mom would cut the grass in her cut-off jean shorts and wife beater t-shirt, her hair in a messy bun. Afterwards she would sit on the stairs to the deck with an ice-cold beer while smelling the fresh cut grass. I'd sit next to her with my Kool-Aid, and we would sit in silence and admire her work.

My dad was always working. He worked third shift at the water plant in town and often worked doubles. He knew my potential and told me, "Em, when you graduate high school, you won't have to worry about anything. You will have the money you need to go to college." I loved my dad very much and I admired that drive in him to take care of his family, but I could see that life, in general, was taking a toll on him. He was young yet, his flock of black hair was peppered with gray, and he had dark circles under his eyes. When he walked, he was hunched over, and it looked as if the weight of the world was on his shoulders.

Submerged

Living with my mom wasn't easy. Since that incident when I was eight, I knew something wasn't right with her. My mom would hallucinate, and she didn't know what was real and what wasn't. She often heard voices that told her to do things that a normal person wouldn't do. She would volunteer at the school and would get into confrontations with the other moms. She was always accusing them of talking about her. One day she clocked Misty Sutherland's mom in the face for looking at her the wrong way. Her paranoia always got the best of her and eventually I was left with no friends and no party invitations. The girls in my school shunned me and often ignored me. Even Sarah, who had been my very best friend since I could walk. She lived across the street, and we would always play together and make forts outside. We would play mail and I would write her letters and she would write back, and we would put them in each other's home mailboxes as if we were far away pen pals. Sarah's mom put a stop to that when Sarah came over one day, and found my mom passed out drunk. One time my mom insisted that someone was roaming around our home during the day, stalking her. I often caught her talking to herself, as if answering a question.

When I was ten years old my mother had a nervous breakdown. I got home from school, and no one was home. This wasn't unusual. I had my own key and I let myself in and prepared a snack. I had assumed she was at the store. The hours and minutes passed by, and I started to get worried. I called my dad at work, but he had been working on some issues at the plant and was unable to take the call.

5

Later, that evening, the police brought her home. They found her roaming the streets in her bra and underwear talking to herself. When approached she became combative and insisted someone from the CIA was following her. Typically, in any other city they most likely would've locked her up for indecent exposure and reckless behavior, however being where we lived, and her history of odd behavior, they drove her home. Word got around to my father. He met them in the driveway, and he immediately took her to the hospital.

The psychiatrist increased her medications, essentially erasing the woman I once knew. Most of the time she took her meds as she was instructed, however the urge for alcohol often led her to a relapse in mental instabilities. When I turned sixteen, I wanted to get a job. I wanted to have a life outside of home and school and I wanted to save for college and maybe make some friends. I envied the girls at school. Sitting together at lunch, talking, and laughing about boys. I wanted to be a part of their world. I wanted to have a friend to confide in and talk to. With my dad working third shift he didn't feel comfortable with leaving my mom alone at night. He agreed that I could work if it was immediately after school for a few short hours. He also paid for my driver's education and said he was going to get me a car. He stated, "Your mom can no longer drive and it's about time you had a car of your own." It wasn't anything fancy. It was a red Honda Civic he bought used from one of his co-workers, but it was mine.

Submerged

Over the years it became too much for my father to bear. I saw less and less of him. I came home from school near the end of my senior year of high school to find a note on my pillow.

My Dearest Em,

I want to first start by telling you how very proud I am of you. I'm just very tired, and I don't know how to deal with your mother any longer. You are old enough now to understand and to take care of yourself. Enclosed is a cashier's check. This is everything I set aside for you over the last ten years. You are very smart, Em, and this should help with any college expenses you may have outside of your scholarship. Find a way for yourself. Become the writer you always wanted to be. I know leaving you is going to hurt, but I hope you will understand.

All my love,

Dad

I couldn't blame him; I know it was a hard life for him. Working and taking care of me and my mother, but I couldn't help but be angry as well. "I hope you will understand?" *That's all I get? Shit, this was a hard life for me as well.* I knew now, more than ever, that my future depended only on me.

Later that evening I prepared dinner. My mother's medications made her very drowsy and sometimes almost comatose. She was no longer that bright, sun kissed, full of vigor mom that I only knew on

7

occasion. She was a shell of mental instability. She approached the table and sat down. She was disheveled and she was drooling. This was a side effect of her medications. I put her plate in front of her. She looked up at me with tears in her eyes, wiped her mouth and quietly asked, "He's gone, isn't he?"

"Yes. He left and he is gone. I will be gone soon too. I have been accepted to Ohio State with a full scholarship and daddy left me some money. I have six months before I leave."

I didn't want to sound harsh, but I was hurting inside, and I couldn't hide my anger and sadness any longer. My anger was more focused on my father who left us at a time when we both needed him the most. I had no right to take it out on her, however all these years I held my tongue out of respect for my parents only to be turned away and left behind. This was the cornerstone of my youth. I would be going away to college, and I couldn't stand the thought of having to give that up to carry the burden of taking care of my mom.

"We need to get you right. I am depending on you mom. Don't give up on yourself! I have never asked you for anything. I never expected anything from you either, but I need you to be well before I go. Please do this for me. Please! I want to be able to go to college and create a fresh start for myself and my future. I can only do this if I know you are okay."

I knew there was nothing we could do about her schizophrenia. That was the card that she was dealt in life many years ago. She

8

needed to take control of her drinking. It only exacerbated her disease and interacted with her medications.

The next day I stayed home from school at the request of my mother, and she asked if I would drive her to a psychiatric/rehab facility. She checked in for ninety days. I continued going to school and taking care of myself. It wasn't anything I didn't already know how to do. I had been doing it on my own since I was ten. I knew that this was the first step of many that my mom would take to make me proud of her.

With my mom in a facility and being looked after I was able to rest peacefully at night and get the much-needed sleep that my mind and body needed for so long. I went to school, and I filled my nights doing what I loved best. Writing. I already started my first novel and set of short stories. My mom was my muse for the first set of short stories. I visited her in rehab regularly. Her strength and her resilience inspired me and showed me what a beautiful person she was. I was seeing another side to her. She was so nurturing and loving. There was another patient in the facility who was her roommate. She was very young. Just a year older than me. She had come from a troubled home and started drinking at the age of fourteen. She had been sexually traumatized and had to struggle with so many obstacles. She faced more struggles than any child should have to endure. My mother embraced her as if she were her own child and took her under her wing. Her name was Maggie. On visits I would always take dinner for my mom and Maggie, and we would sit outside in the garden and talk.

For a moment I resented her and my father because I had wished she had gotten the help she needed earlier so that I would have had a more normal childhood. I would have had the mother figure that she offered Maggie, but I will take this. I will take her lovely spirit and embrace her.

****

It was only a three-hour drive to Ohio State. It was a beautiful Friday morning. The sky was clear, the sun was radiant, and there was a slight breeze. My mother had been as well as expected. Her medications were adjusted again, and she got a job as a dispatcher at the police station. She had been sober for several months and she was grateful for the opportunity to work. Especially given her history in town. She had made good friends who were close by, and she had a sponsor that was there whenever she needed. This was the longest she had been sober and, I was comfortable with leaving as scheduled. I promised to call her regularly and check in. I could drive home on the weekends if she needed me. I hugged her, and she hugged me tight. It was a long hug, and tears were shed. I was proud of her and she in turn was proud of me. I knew she was still on her journey, but for the first time I didn't doubt her ability to keep her word. As I pulled out of the gravel driveway, I saw my mother in my rearview mirror and she waved and smiled, tears still falling from her eyes. I had only wished my father were standing there as well.

Submerged

I was anxious to meet my new roommate. I had few friends back home. Everyone knew my mom and none of the kids invited me to parties and such because of that. I had hoped that college would be my opportunity to find that lifelong bestie. I wasn't looking to party every weekend, but I wanted to experience college life. Especially since I was low key in high school and kept my head in the books. My focus then was getting where I am now. I decided it was okay to live a little if the opportunity presented itself.

I was surprised to have been the first one to arrive at the dorm. I started unpacking and hoped she wouldn't mind which bed I chose. I used the money my dad left me to get new bedding and decorations for my half of the room. Just as I was finishing, she entered the room in all her glory. She had an older gentleman in a suit bringing in her things as if we were at the Ritz Carlton. She was stunning. Her skin reminded me of honey. Soft yet glowing, as if she spent her summer in the Caribbean. Her long brunette locks bounced effortlessly with each step she took. At first, I tensed up. I didn't know how she was going to react to a small-town girl in ripped jeans and chucks. But she was excited and hugged me right away as if she already knew me.

"Isn't this exciting? She said with the enthusiasm of a high school cheerleader.

"How long have you been here? I couldn't wait to get here to meet you. My name is Tonya. You 're adorable! There is a party tonight and we are going!" She didn't even stop to breathe.

Submerged

I was elated. I took to her energy immediately as if the wall flower in me was now blossoming. She didn't know where I came from, and she didn't know who I was. It was a clean slate for me.

"I'm Emily. You can call me Em."

Together we unpacked our things and got ready for our first college party.

Who was I kidding, this was my first party ever.

I could tell Tonya had fashion sense. She let me borrow her clothes and she helped me with my make-up. We laughed and talked.

Tonya told me how her high school sweetheart was also on campus. He got a football scholarship and she followed along. They had been together since being Sophomores in high school. She said we would be meeting up with him and his new roommate.

I was feeling good. I never had alcohol before, yet Tonya was no stranger to it. She pulled out the Tito's and coke and poured us another drink. We jacked up the volume on the stereo to "Whoomp! there it is" and had fun being girls. Initially I was nervous to drink. I saw what it had done to my mother, and I vowed to never let that happen to me, but now in this moment, I felt good. I was happy. I couldn't wait to go to this party.

The late summer breeze felt good on my skin. The walk to the party wasn't far at all. There had been a blazing bonfire and embers of paper cascaded through the air. I was mesmerized by the forked flames

and the heat that radiated off them. Once we rounded the corner Tonya
let out a squeal and went running into the arms of a burly college boy.
I was a bit overwhelmed by the excitement of everything and I could
feel the effects of the vodka. While Tonya was groping her man, his
roommate came over to me and said hi. He introduced himself as
Steven. I can't remember what I said, I may have introduced myself,
but my stomach was not feeling too hot, and I only remember
throwing up.

I was beyond embarrassed. He tenderly grabbed my arm and
sat me down under an oak tree and handed me a bottle of water. The
air smelled of burnt wood and smoke, and there were people all around
laughing, drinking, and taking in one of the last days of summer. I was
nauseous and my head was spinning. What a way to make a first
impression. I apologized profusely and thanked him at the same time
for getting me water. Once I started to feel better, I began to realize
just how attractive Steven was. He had a moderate build with wavy
brown hair. He had the most beautiful green eyes, and they bared a
gleam of kindness. His hands felt soft and smooth. He caressed my
arm, and his touch sent shivers throughout my body. In that moment I
envisioned him holding me close and wrapping his strong arms around
me. I've never felt the touch of a boy. I never had a boyfriend. This
was unfamiliar territory for me. I didn't know how to react around him
at first. It was a lot to process, but somehow just his gentle touch left
me breathless. His soul and his genuine nature made it easy for me to

relax and be me. We sat there as Tonya and Jacob were off canoodling, unaffected by the fact that I threw up for dear life.

Steven and I talked deep into the night. I could tell he was unlike any other guy I had seen or had a crush on before. I loved his Boston accent. He told me about his family, and I told him about mine. I admired his tenacity to go out on his own and forget the comforts which his family could provide for him. It reminded me of my dad in the sense that Steven wanted to work for what was his. He didn't want it to be given to him. The cherry on top was when he informed me his major would be English Literature. What are the odds? I wasn't expecting it, but I could see how sensitive he was and how seriously he took school and this opportunity to be there.

His smile was warm, and it may sound premature, but never in a million years would I think I would have met my soul mate night one at college.

STEVEN

The pinnacle of my independence was contingent on succeeding on my own and not under the influence and power of my family. Especially my father. I took the initiative and threw myself into my studies all through high school so that I could achieve a full scholarship on my own. My friends thought I was crazy. What they didn't realize is once I graduated, I would move far away, and I could pursue a future of my own and not one which was destined for me. At least that was the plan.

My parents weren't what I would call romantically happy. They were socially happy. Don't get me wrong, they were best friends, but they were both living under the expectations that their parents laid out for them. To the outside they seemed like the happiest of couples; however, once home and away from the spotlight they both retired to their separate bedrooms. It was more like an arrangement than a marriage. They were both content and seemed pleased with their life. They were both amazing parents and did what they could to ensure we grew up with everything we needed and more. I just wanted something different. I had an older sister Paige. When Paige was in elementary school my parents noticed behavioral changes in her and she seemed socially inapt. She had Asperger's Syndrome. Much focus was placed on Paige, and I was just expected to be the golden child. The one who would take over when the time was right for my dad to retire. No one took into consideration what I wanted. I guess that's how it worked when you were a part of a family with status.

I was accepted to Ohio State University. My father was not pleased. Per his request I was to attend Harvard and study law. His plan was for me to run the business after he stepped down. My heart wasn't into law. I wanted a fresh start somewhere else and on my own. Away from professors who knew generations of my family and who looked at the sizeable grants and donations that had been contributed over the years. I earned a full ride scholarship. All my high school years as president of student counsel, obtaining a GPA of 4.0 as well as the weekends of volunteer work within the community paid off. I essentially gave up my teen years to earn my own way and now I looked forward to meeting new people, exploring the Midwest, and getting into a fraternity. I couldn't wait to go to a college football game.

I was beyond ecstatic to be on my way. I was free. I chose to major in English literature. The furthest thing from law. I was taking my independence seriously but would later find out that sometimes fait leads you back to where you started.

As a first-year student I lived on campus in the dorms. Since My father was completely against me going to Ohio State, he didn't bother to arrange my travels. My mother didn't want to create any waves, so she just wished me well and sent me on my way. I decided, rather than fly, I would drive. Alone I went on an 11.5-hour car ride from Boston to Columbus. Only stopping for gas and essentials. I didn't want to waste any time.

When I arrived my roommate, Jacob Mahoning, was already getting settled. Both his parents and his younger sister were in tow to wish him well. We clicked right away when I saw him roll his eyes behind his mother's back. He couldn't wait for them to leave. On the one hand I was embarrassed for him yet on the other I envied that kind of love. Once the emotional tirade left, we were left to our own devices. Of course, word already got around about a party. Not even twenty-four hours in and we were well on our way to college life. It was a Friday night, and classes didn't start until Monday. Let the party begin.

Jacob had told me he was here on a football scholarship and against his wishes his high school sweetheart decided to attend as well. In Jacob's own words, "Tonya came from money. She could go anywhere she wanted to." It's not that he didn't love Tonya, but this is the only girl he had been with since he was sixteen. He had thought college life would give them an opportunity for new experiences, but he couldn't bring himself to break it off with her.

I wasn't going to inject myself into that situation, especially since I just met the guy. I wasn't much for the drama of relationships. I had no qualms about breaking up with my girlfriend, Monica, for my future. I was here for new beginnings.

17

Submerged

Before leaving for the party, we chugged a few beers and I was feeling good.

When we got there, we saw a massive bonfire. I poured another beer from the nearest Keg and made my way through the crowd with Jacob. Finally, he spotted Tonya, and we walked over. She was beautiful. Honestly, I was quite surprised. They didn't mesh at all, and I knew the type. With her was a petite girl. She looked lost and like she may have had too much to drink already.

Tonya jumped up on Jacob and wrapped her skinny thighs around his waist. You could tell she already had a few drinks, and she was pouring on the PDA. It was a bit uncomfortable, not only for me but for the other girl as well. I walked over to her and introduced myself.

"Hi, I'm Steven, Jacob's roommate."

"Hey, I'm Em. This is wild right? It's a lot to take in for one day. I just got here this afternoon. How about you?"

"Same."

The brief silence was deafening and a bit awkward, but something drew me to her. It was if something fell into place. I couldn't describe it. She was cute and she had a way about her that looked like home. She was short, maybe 5'3". Her hair was very dark, almost black and it was poker straight. Her face was round, and she had high cheek bones that reminded me of apples. She had full lips,

18

and she was a natural beauty. This intrigued me and made me want to get to know her more. Everything around us seemed to be muted. I thought she was going to say something, and, at that moment, she just threw up everywhere!

I was stunned, but at the same time the only way I knew how to react was to sit her down under a nearby tree and give her a bottle of water. This girl whom I had barely known was now the center of my attention and all I wanted to do was take care of her.

Soon she started to feel better, and we talked all night. Much to my surprise she was also majoring in English literature. She told me about her home life. How she was an only child and her father left because of her mother's illness and addiction to alcohol. In this one night I felt comfort that I had never known before. We gave each other our undivided attention. Nothing was forced and the conversation was easy. I wasn't expecting to meet anyone tonight. I wasn't expecting to find my future.

TOGETHER

From that first night we were inseparable. When you saw me, you saw Steven and vice versa. We were both determined to graduate with honors. Our goals for the future aligned and we were always on the same page. By the end of our sophomore year much had changed. We both moved out of our dorms and got an apartment together. Tonya and Jacob were no longer an item, and Tonya eventually dropped out and moved back home. Steven got word that his father was very ill. He suffered from pancreatic cancer. This sent shock waves through the family, and it created a sense of urgency to get someone ready to take over the firm. Steven immediately prepared for and took his LSAT and changed his major from English literature to Law. This changed the entire trajectory of our college life. I would graduate prior to Steven. He would have an additional three years of law school after completing his four years for his undergraduate degree and then he would need to take the bar exam. I had no idea what was going to happen once I graduated. We didn't talk about our future and whether we would be together.

One weekend a month we would drive to see my mom. She was doing well for herself. She met a new guy, Terry. He was a bit of a hippie and a tree hugger, but that was good for her. He introduced her to yoga and meditation. Terry was a horticulturist and soon he moved in with her and they planted the most amazing garden.

Submerged

My mom loved Steven and he in turn cared deeply for her. He called her mom. He often talked about how he missed his own mom. Even though they talked regularly, it wasn't the same. In addition, with his dad's chemotherapy treatments, his mother had her hands full. They had the means to hire a full-time nurse, and they did, but Steven's mother never left her husband's side. Once a month Steven flew to Boston from Columbus to spend time with his family. We didn't know how much time his dad had left. We had been told that pancreatic cancer was aggressive.

Near the end of my senior year in college Steven got a phone call to come home. Just hours after his plane landed his father passed away. I flew to Boston on the next available flight to be near him during this time. I had only just met his parents recently. The fate of the business and the family fell on Steven. Decisions needed to be made, and I could sense that the pressure was more than Steven could endure.

Steven insisted I return to school. He stated he would be back within the next couple of weeks. Against my better judgement I did. I had always promised myself I would put myself first. I worked hard to get where I was. In addition to graduating with my degree in English Literature, I had a literary agent and was well on my way to having my first fictional novel published. Things were looking good for me. I didn't think anything would ever get in the way of the relationship we had.

21

Submerged

Two weeks turned into a month. There were legal issues to take care of and of course it was the matter of the Board at his father's law firm. We rarely spoke. Between my studies and everything Steven needed to take care of at home, I was lucky to speak to him once a week. It was near graduation, and I had many decisions to make. I couldn't stay in Columbus forever and my agent was already talking about how much of a success they were anticipating my book to be. I had received a sizeable advance and couldn't believe my first novel got picked so quickly. I had established myself with short stories and publications throughout college. With all of this, I felt like my head was going to explode. I decided to walk to the library and get a change of scenery and some fresh air. The apartment was dark and lonely. It just wasn't the same without Steven. While everything was going right, I missed him terribly and it felt like a piece of me was missing.

I was lost in my studies at the library and before I knew it, it was almost 8:00. While walking home I stopped at the corner Chinese restaurant and picked up my favorite orange chicken and fried rice. I walked into the apartment, it was dark, but there was a solitary candle burning on the kitchen table. Within the silhouette of the flame sat Steven. He stood up when he saw me, and I jumped into his arms. We were silent for what felt like several minutes. We embraced until he whispered in my ear, "I love you so much Em."

His hands slowly caressed my neck as he stared at me. I knew he wanted me- his piercing green eyes looking into my soul. His hands were soft and cool, and they crept down my arms and around my waist where he pulled me in tight and pressed his soft lips against mine, gently sliding his tongue into my mouth. I wanted him. I liked this. The slowness of his touch and the way he breathed every ounce of me in. I missed him. I wanted him. He pulled my skirt slowly up and lifted me onto the counter. His fingers slid into the part of me that longed for his touch. Slowly he moved his fingers in and out of me and instructed me to look at him.

"Does it feel good?" he whispered.

I moaned. A deep sultry moan and replied, "Yes. I want you. I want you now."

In that moment he picked me up and took me to our bed. He thrusted himself into me. He felt good. It was like he was molded for my body. I took every inch of him in and squeezed into it so he could feel me. All of me.

We were back to being us. Together.

****

Before we knew it, it was my graduation day. My mom and Terry drove into Columbus. Steven insisted on inviting his mom Vivian, and Paige. They were meeting for the first time and from what I could tell everyone enjoyed each other's company. It was a gorgeous day and Steven had reserved a spot at the park for all of us afterwards to celebrate. He ordered food from our favorite BBQ place. We didn't really discuss what was going to happen after I graduated. I think we were both avoiding it. He still had a few years left of school and in his father's will, he had indicated, Steven would not receive any type of inheritance unless he not only took over the law firm, but he had to move back home to Boston to be near his mother and sister. I had not intended to move to Boston unless I had assurance that our future would be solid.

The graduation ceremony was lovely, and we all headed to the park. To my surprise there was a tethered hot air balloon.

"What in the world? Steven, did you do this?"

"I thought I would take my favorite girl on a trip to the clouds. What do you say, Em?"

"Yes, of course!" I was beaming with excitement.

My mom, Terry, Viv, and Paige were grinning from ear to ear. It was as if they knew this was going to happen. I thought I saw my mom's eyes water. She waved at me to go ahead and said, "Don't worry about us, we're going to eat some of this fabulous food."

Steven and I boarded the balloon. I had flutters in my stomach and was beyond excited. It was the perfect day to take flight. Steven wrapped his arms around me from behind as we soared higher and higher. Once we reached our designated height, Steven was handed a box from the balloonist.

No- this is not happening. He turned to me and opened the box. There was the most stunningly beautiful emerald cut diamond staring at me and I could barely breathe.

"Em, When I am with you, I feel like I can fly. I feel like I can do anything with you by my side. With all the uncertainties that lie ahead this is the one thing of which I am sure. Will you do me the honor of becoming my wife?"

"YES!!!!" I could barely contain myself.

When the balloon landed, my mom ran to me with her arms wide open. She knew all along.

"My sweet Emily. How far you have come. All your dreams are coming true. I am so incredibly proud of you and so fortunate and blessed to have a daughter like you, and now a son.

Submerged

26

Chapter 2

Change

EMILY

Within the next few months, we moved to Boston and into the family home with Viv and Paige and started planning our wedding. I hated that I would be so far away from my mom, but with Steven transferring to Harvard and the money from his family, money was not an object. I could fly mom and Terry to Boston whenever she wanted to visit, and I could go home to Ohio as well.

The Van Aken home was massive and gave one a sense of nobility when walking into it. It had been in the family for generations and on a scale replicated a small castle. It was Tudor style and came complete with a roundabout driveway in the front. In the center there is a grandiose fountain. The gardens were spectacular and soon became one of my most favorite features of the home. They were green and lush with pops of color everywhere. They brought a sense of serenity and peace. I never realized the amenities Steven had. It was weird having a butler and a housekeeper. I was a very independent person and sometimes it drove me crazy to have someone run my bath water or bring me my coffee. I underestimated the amount of old money Steven's family really had. Money was never a concern. At this time, my world seemed perfect.

Vivian offered to pay for our wedding. She insisted on giving us as much as we needed to wow society. The Van Aken's were very prominent and well known. They had politicians and celebrities close to the family and she wanted to ensure they were included on the guest list. I wasn't used to having this type of attention, but I quickly learned that I could become accustomed to it. Viv and I got along, and I looked to her as a second mother. She was a very loyal woman. She cared deeply for her family and ensured that family was always a priority. Viv had planned a trip for myself, her, and my mother to find the perfect dress. On that day as we waited for my mom at the airport, Viv expressed to me how this would be the only wedding she would get to plan. It had been difficult with Paige and coming to terms with the fact that she wouldn't be like many of her friends' daughters. She knew Paige wouldn't have much of a normal life and this saddened her. Paige was such a beautiful and quiet woman; but she was extremely introverted and grew up with her mom as her only friend. Vivian had tried to join groups with other children with Asperger's, but Paige was so reclused and often it would create a sense of trauma within her. Eventually Vivian realized that she would have to let it go and accept the life that was planned out for Paige. Paige and I got along well. I knew my boundaries with her. I enjoyed the silence, and we would often just sit together in the gardens and admire nature. Our relationship wasn't forced. It was natural.

It sounds cliche, but my wedding day was a day of fairytales. Everything was perfect. Each detail and each moment were flawless. We were married at the Aldine Castle in Brookline. Over four hundred guests were in attendance and the air was full of romance. It was a perfect spring day. Clear blue skies, not a cloud in sight. There was a soft gentle breeze, but combined with the warm hug from the sun, the temperature was exactly right. I wore a beautiful Vera Wang gown in light ivory. It was a strapless dress, and it had a sweetheart neckline, Chantilly lace and hand-sewn crystal beading. The bottom of the dress itself was like a ball gown, delicately cinched at the waist with gorgeous rouching. The veil was made of the same Chantilly lace that was embedded in my dress. I felt elegant. I felt sexy. My maid of honor and bridesmaid were Tonya and Paige. They each wore a long-sleeved dress in deep plum with a plunging neckline and a sexy slit up the front. They carried fragrant bouquets of fresh lilacs with an abundance of beautiful green leaves. My mother walked me down the aisle as I wouldn't have it any other way. My mom and I had been through too much for me not to give her the honor of giving me away. Steven couldn't take his eyes off me. As I got closer, I handed Tonya my bouquet and looked into his eyes. He took my hands in his and he whispered, "you look stunning." I was elated when the pastor announced us husband and wife and I was now, officially, a Van Aken.

After the bridal party photos, we made our grand entrance on the balcony of the Modern club. The ceiling was donned with gold leaf and hanging from it were crystal chandeliers. The walls were paneled with dark mahogany wood and the rays of sunshine were radiating through the large picture windows. Lilac centerpieces filled the room with spring flares, and I felt like we were dancing in a royal garden. We drank the best champagne and danced until our feet hurt. Our wedding was on the front page of every newspaper in Boston, and it was the event of the year. The Pièce de resistance was that my best friend Tonya and Steven's best man Jacob rekindled their love and within time they were married as well. Our bonds were so close that they moved to Boston to be near us.

Years passed and Steven passed the bar exam. Finally, it was time to search for a home of our own. We were still living with Viv and Paige. We had discussed staying where we were in the family home. I loved being around Steven's family; and even though we had our own wing in the home I was ready for something to call our own. We had wanted something that would be close to the Van Aken estate. The task of finding a new home was primarily on me. Steven had finally taken over the firm and he was in the process of hiring new lawyers. He wanted to bring new talent to the firm. While he kept those that had worked with his father and had been established, he wanted to make the firm his own. This ruffled feathers but at the end of the day Steven had the final say.

There had been a very modest sized modern style cape cod home that I had been eyeing for a while. Ironically, it was only two blocks away from Viv and Paige and it recently hit the market. It was only a quarter of the size of the Van Aken estate, but it was more than enough for Steven and me. We were hoping to start a family, so I wanted something with ample space for the children and I always dreamed of having a large back porch with a porch swing. Like the Van Aken estate, it had a gated turnaround drive, and beautiful gardens. As soon as I walked through the doors, I felt like I was at home. Everything was pristine and new. It was only five years old, and the current owners had to sell as they were relocating due to work. The cabinetry and bookshelves were just as I would have chosen. It was as if this home was just waiting for me to walk through its doors. I was most enamored with all the natural sunlight that illuminated the home. It made the home feel warm and cozy.

Within four months of moving into our new home we found out we were expecting. Everything was happening just as it should. We were in our new home, and I had hired an interior decorator for the nursery. Steven was working late nights. It was taking him time to get acclimated to the firm and he was in a position where he had to prove himself. The board was not too thrilled with all the changes Steven made and they tried to push him out but between him and his mother they had full control. Steven just wanted to prove he could do it and live up to the expectation that was handed to him. I was able to finish my second novel. It was in the printing stage and, in a few months, would be on shelves everywhere. My agent, Gary, started talking about book signings and travel. With the baby on the way, I didn't think that would be possible. The algorithm of life doesn't have a plan. There is no order. Don't get me wrong, I was thankful for my life, but at the same time I felt like I didn't have a second to breathe. I was so consumed with getting the house together, finishing my book, and just being exhausted from pregnancy; that I didn't realize the lack of time and intimacy between Steven and myself. The time seemed to go so fast and before I knew it our little one was well on her way to enter the world.

Steven had hired a new lawyer at the firm. Monica. They knew each other in high school and per Steven she was very knowledgeable and offered the expertise he needed. I wasn't the jealous type, and it didn't bother me that he hired a female until Tonya started chirping in my ear. I loved that she lived twenty minutes away but there were times when she drove me crazy. Especially during my pregnancy. She had been upset that we weren't pregnant at the same time. She and Jacob had issues conceiving, but I kept reassuring her that it would happen when the time was right. I had the impression that she was jealous, and I chalked her annoying accusations up to her vague attempt to bring me down.

"Em, how do you know what they're doing when they're at the office for that extended amount of time? It seems like every time I talk to you, he is at the office. Do the two of you ever see each other?"

These conversations with Tonya were exhausting. Between Tonya and my hormones, I lost it.

Steven came home late one night, and I was fully prepared to confront him. Just as I was about to speak, I felt sharp pain radiate from my back into my belly. It was unlike anything I had ever felt. Within 2 minutes I had another one. Steven asked me what was wrong.

"I think I'm having contractions."

We timed them and when they got to be around one-minute apart we called my doctor. She told us to head to the hospital and check in at labor and delivery.

Eight hours later we were welcoming our sweet Lulu into the world. She was the most precious baby I had ever laid eyes on. Ten fingers, ten toes, a small patch of curly brown hair, and the sweetest smile I ever saw. By this time all the emotions and worry I felt beforehand were gone. Lulu was all I focused on. I felt silly for even thinking I was on the brink of asking Steven if he had been having an affair.

STEVEN

I missed my dad. We didn't always get along. Now that I was about to be a father, I understood him more and had wished he were here. I knew the best way to honor him was to do what he needed me to do and that was to take over the firm. It isn't what I wanted, but sometimes in life we must do what is necessary. It would be lucrative, and I would be able to provide for Emily as my father provided for us. She needed to have the best, and I could offer that to her.

When I married Em I didn't think life could get any better. She was amazing. I was blown away watching her walk down the aisle. It was as if she took the breath right out of me. She became my world. She didn't care what anyone else thought of her. She had an air of confidence about her, and she was one of the most creative people I knew. Her stories and her novels just mesmerized me. She often carried a journal with her whenever we were out, and she told me that sometimes a place or a moment would inspire her, and she would need to write it down. It provided inspiration for her stories. I appreciated that about her. Always dreaming and always living her life as she wanted it to be lived. This motivated me and encouraged me to embrace the life which was given to me and appreciate what I was given and what I was born into. Marrying Emily was the best choice I had ever made, and I never questioned it. It was natural having her by my side and I couldn't wait to start a family with her.

Submerged

When I became a lawyer, I was thrusted into this whirlwind to get things going at the firm. Pressure was on me, and decisions needed to be made. Many of the lawyers were within retirement age and it consisted of all men. Men who golfed with my father and quite frankly were set in their ways. We didn't have a single female lawyer at the firm, and this bothered me, especially since we were starting to take on medical cases that involved women and women issues. One of the first items on my agenda was to hire a female lawyer. I contacted a headhunter who could acquire what I was looking for. It was now my firm, and I was making decisions based on what the needs were for all of us.

The first name on the list was Monica Anderson. She graduated at the top of her class and had nearly a perfect score on the Bar exam. I knew Monica. I hesitated to even review her resume; but I needed to set personal feelings and issues aside for the benefit of the firm. We needed the best and if she was the best then I needed to hire her. I arranged an interview.

Em was eight months pregnant, and we were ecstatic for the arrival of our little girl. I know how Emily wanted to be a mother. Her pregnancy hadn't been easy. From what I understood most women are only sick during their first trimester; however, Em had been sick throughout. She did a lot of tossing and turning and waking up throughout the night. I would wake with her but she insisted I go back to bed until finally she suggested I move into the spare room so I could get my rest. We hadn't made love in months, and I often turned to porn and a bottle of lotion to fulfill my desires. My commute to the office was twenty minutes so I would drive home at lunch to check on her and make sure she was feeling okay. Today I stopped at the florists to get a bouquet of white roses. Em's favorite. I also stopped at our favorite bakery and picked up their famous brownies. Emily craved chocolate while pregnant. She often couldn't hold much food down, but sweets stuck with her. I teased her and would say it was because of our precious baby girl growing inside of her, already spoiled. When I got home Emily was asleep on the sofa. On her side. Emily was very petite. She had grown significantly and sleeping on her back was painful. I could see her swollen feet peeking out from under the blanket and I gently covered them up and brushed my lips on her warm cheeks. I placed her roses in a vase and set them next to the saltines and ginger ale on the table next to the sofa. I delicately placed the ribbon wrapped box of brownies next to it and left to go back to the office. When I returned, I was surprised to hear from my secretary that Monica had already returned my call for an interview. She will be in the office tomorrow at one o clock. This was a good sign. For the first time in a long time, I was hopeful about my career and about taking over the firm. I could now see its potential and all the opportunities we could offer.

****

I was extremely nervous to see Monica. I couldn't sleep. I just kept tossing and turning thinking about her. Thinking about how she felt when I met her in high school. I tossed and turned and stroked my cock thinking about her thick lips wrapped around it. I slept for what felt like two hours. My anxiety had been at an all-time high and I was up and out of the house before Emily even woke. My thoughts raced as I prepared my list of interview questions. She and I had a tumultuous past and I wasn't sure if she was taking this invite for an interview seriously or if she was using it as an opportunity to say what was on her mind. I'm quite sure she had a lot to say. June, my secretary buzzed into my office.

"Your one-o-clock is here. Monica Anderson."

"Thank you, June. I will be right out." I immediately started to perspire, and my hands felt clammy. I composed myself and took a deep breath and headed to the lobby.

Walking down the corridor I could see her. Her beauty catapulted me into a whirlwind of lust and desire. If I'm being honest, I wanted to take her right there. She looked just as I remembered her, only older and sexier. I hadn't seen Monica since my father's funeral. Thinking about our encounter then and seeing her now made me hard and I had to conceal the bulge within my pants. I had to re-focus and center my thoughts on something other than bending her over on my desk.

"Well, well, well, if it isn't Steven Van Aken." She stood from her seat with her leather briefcase in hand and extended her hand out for me to shake it.

"Hello, Monica." I shook her hand and the instant my hand touched hers I felt like a high school boy again. "Let's go to my office. We can talk there."

The firm was growing. We were taking on more cases. This was good except I didn't have the staff to cover the load and I had to prove to myself that I could run the business like a well-oiled rig. My headhunter stated Monica had the recommendations and the skills I was looking for and she was one of the first to show interest. I had to think about the firm. I was in love with Em. She was my soulmate. I wasn't going to destroy that happiness for a few minutes of something I would only regret. In high school, Monica was frivolous and had the maturity of a nat. I fell in love with Emily for her soul and her beauty was a bonus. I couldn't imagine building my life without her. Now we were starting our family and soon we would be welcoming our new baby.

It would seem Monica had no intention of anything other than a place within the firm. When I sat down to talk with her, she was all business. It was as if I was speaking with someone I had never met before. I was, however, enamored with her beauty. Her doe shaped blue eyes and pouty lips. Her blonde locks cascading down her shoulders. Her breasts full but not too revealing. She looked classy. Appropriate for the interview. A hint of mystery behind her clothes even though I knew every inch of her body.

Submerged

Once I could focus on why she was in my office I was able to discuss her resume, experience, and why she felt she would be a good fit within our firm. Of course, it wasn't just up to me. I had to also run it by the board members, but I didn't see why she wouldn't fit in. I already had a couple of cases I was ready to assign to her.

Not once did she mention our past.

She looked over at the photo of a pregnant Emily and myself on my desk. "You look happy Steven. You look good." Monica smiled and I could sense the sincerity in her voice. We could do this. We could work together.

"I'm very happy. I will be in touch once I talk with the board. I will have my secretary call you with an offer. I look forward to working with you." I stood and led her to the door.

"Sounds good. I look forward to hearing from you."

With that Monica was walking out of my office and I was hopeful that we had just landed one of the best lawyers in Boston.

I didn't get home until well past 9:00. Emily was passed out in the lounge chair with her laptop open to her manuscript. I gently aroused her and helped her to bed. I kissed her on the forehead and headed downstairs. I was wide awake and couldn't sleep.

****

The following Monday it was confirmed by the board, and I hired Monica. I was beyond thrilled as this meant the workload could be distributed appropriately. I needed her to start as soon as possible. I would need to take leave when the baby is born. Just a week or two to help Em out and be with the baby. The due date was approaching, and I felt like I was buried with work. Pressure was mounting to succeed and run the firm as my father did. There was no margin of error here. It did not go favorably with the board when they were notified, I would be taking leave.

I had an office cleared for her. One of the best with a view of downtown Boston. It's the least I could do. Our past didn't end on good terms and I felt I at least owed her that. If she played her cards right, she could make partner.

She started the day after she accepted the position. I wanted to ensure that I arrived earlier than usual so that I could welcome her and make her feel as comfortable as possible. One of her first cases was assisting me. I needed her skillset. I had just taken on a case of several women suing a pharmaceutical company for their IUD device which caused severe uterine damage and organ failure. Our firm was all men, and I needed a women's touch on this one. It was a sensitive subject and all three of these women are now sterile and unable to have children. I felt Monica could approach this case with the sensitivity needed.

Early mornings and late nights ensued. In the beginning it was all business. I focused on the tasks at hand and was able to control my sexual desires to ravish her. Weeks in and the nights became later, and soon we were spending between ten and twelve hours together a day. I found myself enjoying our conversations and on occasion I caught glimpses of her staring my way. It felt good to be looked at again. It felt good to be treated like a man. She had expressed that she was dating some guy. She never indicated to me what his name was; however, I could tell it wasn't as serious as she made it seem. I would be lying if I said it didn't bother me. The more she talked about him the more I found myself becoming jealous. Quite silly, but I realized that I was forming feelings for her. We were never intimate. Not in the beginning. I was forming an emotional connection with her, and it was one I wasn't sure I would be able to let go.

Angela, Emily's mother, had come to stay with us in the final stretch of her pregnancy. Sometime had gone by and we only had three weeks until the due date. Being at work with Monica was a nice distraction. Em had been on edge for months and it was difficult being in the same room with her. It was always tense and stressful. I did what I could, but she was so hormonal and grumpy all the time.

Monica came into the office one morning and knocked on my door.

"Can I talk with you for a minute?" She looked ominous and I can tell something was on her mind.

"Of Course, come on in." I got the sense that what would come next was not going to be pleasant.

"I was wondering if you wouldn't mind if I took a week off. I know you will be off soon with the new baby and well, my boyfriend planned a trip to the Bahamas. With all the late hours at work we haven't had much time together and he expressed to me that he is concerned that if we don't start seeing each other more that he may need to end the relationship."

"I see. Well of course you can have time off." I was hesitant. It's not that I didn't want her to have the time, it was that I knew she would be with him, and I wouldn't get to be near her.

"Are you sure?" She inched closer. I could feel the heat radiating from her. She put her hand on my arm and was staring into my eyes. I stared back and I could feel myself wanting to wrap my arms around her. It felt like she wanted me to tell her to stay. She leaned in and pressed her lips onto mine then slowly slid her tongue inside my mouth.

I wanted her. I kissed her back, and gently pushed her away. We stared at each other for a moment, and I knew if we were somewhere other than work, I would be taking all of her.

"I'm so sorry Steven. I thought, well, I thought you wanted it too."

"Monica, I want you. I want all of you. I want nothing more than to slam my office door and rip your clothes off. I think of you constantly, but I am married and in a couple of weeks I am having a child." God, I wanted her. I turned away and ran my fingers through my hair hesitating before I spoke. "I think that if you take this trip and get away for a while that will be good for you. For us. Enjoy your time and do what you can to focus on yourself." I couldn't look at her as I said the words.

She placed her hand on my back. "Are you sure? I want you too. And I know I'm not supposed to have these feelings for you. You have a life and a beautiful wife, but I feel so connected to you. You're right. We need this break." I turned around and she stepped aside, and I could see her eyes welling up with tears.

"If it's okay I'm going to head home early." She turned and walked out of my office.

That evening as I headed home, I received a text from her that she was heading out the next day. Her flight was leaving in the morning, and she would return in approximately seven days.

I didn't respond.

The next seven days I was a wreck. I left the office every day at five o clock and had dinner with Em and her mom. I tried my best to focus on Emily and eventually I got into the rhythm of things with her again. She was glowing and even though she felt miserable she was the most beautiful woman I had ever seen. She always smiled even when she felt like shit. I knew how excited she was. I lay on the couch with her in the evenings and I would rub her feet and we would talk into the night.

"I know I haven't been myself Steven. I promise once our little one comes, I will be back to normal. I didn't realize how exhausting being pregnant would be. There isn't enough yoga in the world to prepare me for this. You must think I look like a cow. "

I could tell she had been feeling down and I suppose my absence hadn't been easy for her. I missed a lot of her pregnancy trying to get things in order with the firm and with my late nights with Monica working on cases.

"I haven't been myself lately either, Em. I'm sorry about that. This whole experience is new for both of us and with everything going on at work I didn't take your feelings into consideration. I hope you can forgive me." I was sorry for the time lost with Em due to work, but deep down I wasn't sorry for the feelings I had developed for Monica.

I was surprised to see Monica beat me to the office the following Monday. I passed her while I was walking in, and she was grabbing her coffee. Her skin was sun-kissed and glowing. The smell of coconut and pineapple still lingering. She didn't seem to notice me, and I darted for my office. It would be impossible to avoid each other all day. We have a meeting at ten and I needed to go over the up-and-coming cases that needed to be handled while I was out with Emily.

"June, can you make sure the conference room is ready at ten. I'm going to meet with Ms. Anderson there this morning. Please make sure you update the calendar." She glanced up at me from her readers. "Will do Mr. Van Aken."

I decided it was no longer a good idea to hold our meetings in our personal offices. The conference room was in the center of the firm and was surrounded by glass. It was within everyone's eye view. One of the many modern updates I made when taking over. Emily texted me. It read, *may your day be full of positive energy and vibes. All my Love, Em.* I was going to need more than positive energy. I was going to need self-control, but I was thankful she texted me as it put her in the forefront of my thoughts. At least for the moment.

I ended up being late for our meeting. I had a conference call that ran over, and I couldn't get away from it. Monica was waiting, patiently typing away on her laptop and trifling through files which lay next to her. I could tell just by looking at her that she was focused. So much so that she didn't even notice I had entered the room. I placed my laptop and notebook on the table and took a seat, watching her thinking and working. It's as if I could see the gears grinding. Watching her made me smile.

Finally, she looked up. "Steven, hi. I didn't even hear you come in."

"No, don't apologize. I was just watching you." *Don't be weird Steven*, I thought.

"Yeah, that sounds creepy." We both laughed.

"I feel like I'm drowning from all the catch up I am doing. I didn't realize taking a week off would lead to chaos and four cups of coffee." She picked up her mug, and she blew into it trying to calm the steam before slowly sipping the brown concoction.

"Well, I certainly hope that you were able to relax and enjoy your time." I tried to pretend that what happened between us before her departure was just a mistake. An error in judgement. Maybe she forgot.

She stood from her seat on the other side of the table and walked over to me. She sat next to me and looked me in the eyes. *Damn those deep blue eyes!*

"Yes, it did. It also gave me clarity. I don't know what is going on between us, but I know that I am not okay with it just ending. I know that sounds a bit forward. Don't get me wrong I love being with my boyfriend. We talked and we discussed our future together. We both agreed to take it slow. I thought being with him would make me forget about you, but the truth of the matter is it didn't. I know you love Emily and I know you are starting a family, but I am always here for you, I can be here professionally, personally, or both. No strings attached. It will be between us. However, to be clear, I do not want whatever this is between us to interfere with my place here at the firm. I have a reputation to withhold, and I have worked too hard to have this taken away from me. I can keep it strictly business."

I was speechless. I wasn't expecting her to be so forward. If anything, her confidence turned me on instantly.

"Let's continue as we have been, Monica. I appreciate you being up front and open with me, and I am looking forward to what is to come. "

She smiled then went back to her computer and we began the meeting.

Chapter 3
Bewilderment

EMILY

There wasn't anything more magnificent than holding my Lulu. I didn't think it was possible to feel this much love for someone. I loved being a mom and I immediately embraced it.

Steven took a week off after Lulu was born to be home. It was nice reconnecting again and having that time together. We were now a family. Afterwards he was back to being at the office for long hours. At the time, I didn't mind it much. I had our precious little girl to take care of and bond with. I enjoyed our early morning cuddles. After feeding her I would nuzzle my face in her neck and breathe in her sweet baby smell.

Lulu was an exceptional baby. She rarely fussed and she slept throughout the night. I started going to a local mommy and me group to meet new moms and I often felt bad for them as I listen to them talk of their sleepless nights and cranky babies. Eventually I stopped going because I felt like I had nothing to complain about.

I can't really pinpoint when the addiction started. It was a gradual process. Having Lulu made me realize how intensely I could love. There were days when I looked at her and I would sob uncontrollably because I loved her so much. I couldn't believe that this tiny human belonged to me. She had a little bit of me mixed with a bit of Steven. On our quiet nights alone as I held her in my arms I would think about my childhood and question how my mother could waste so much of her time drinking and neglecting me. Allowing me to go on taking care of myself at the young age of ten with no regard for my well-being. Okay, yes, she had a mental disorder as well, but to consciously drink knowing it exacerbated her mental symptoms was mind blowing to me. Stevens' schedule was all over the place. There were weeks when he was home every day by five o'clock and others when I wouldn't see him for days on end because he was home too late and up before me in the mornings. Two ships passing in the night. His schedule was tough especially when cases were in the public eye and demanded a lot of attention.

I was good about filling up my days to pass the time. Lulu always kept me busy. Nights were another story. Nights I would write and catch up on some of my reading. However, I needed another outlet and that's when I would tie the night out with a glass of wine. It became common for me to always have a glass of wine on the back porch prior to going to bed. One glass turned into the whole bottle. I liked the way it made me feel. It allowed me to avoid the issues and the thoughts that were in the forefront of my mind. I started to panic thinking that I also had the same mental illness as my mother. I would get paranoid with thoughts of Steven cheating and losing everything until I realized that if Steven's behavior wasn't so sporadic, I probably wouldn't doubt his fidelity. I could uncheck that box of crazy.

****

Submerged

My book sales were soaring and just as my agent suspected it had made the bestsellers list. It was now time to talk about a book tour. I wasn't sure how Steven would react to that, especially since Lulu was now only six months old. My mom offered to travel with me and help and I loved the idea. After talking with Gary, we decided to limit the tour to five major cities across the United States. Traveling from the East Coast to the West and then working our way back. I anticipated the journey to take about two weeks. When I sat down to talk with Steven about it, he was thrilled with the idea. Frankly, I was surprised. We hadn't spent much time together and it seemed almost as if he couldn't wait for me to go. I guess in the back of my mind I had hoped he would've taken the initiative or suggested to take a couple of weeks off to go with us and support me for a change. I had been very understanding of his workload and schedule; however, my intuition was leading me to a dark place, and I did my best to suppress my feelings.

The tour was a success, and I had a wonderful time reconnecting with my mom and watching her beam over Lulu. She was such a different person from when I was younger, and I was elated to see her dote on Lulu the way that she did.

When we returned home from the tour, I was surprised to see that Steven's car was in the drive. It was a Tuesday, and it was only 2:00. I had taken an early flight hoping I could put together a nice meal and surprise him. The driver carried in our bags, I tipped him, and I immediately headed inside. I could hear Steven talking in the kitchen. As I rounded the doorway, I was shocked to see Monica sitting at the island with a glass of wine. Steven looked surprised to see us. He rushed over to me to grab Lulu and give her a kiss on the forehead.

"Oh, I missed my girl. Monica and I had court all morning. We won our case and came back here to celebrate."

"I see. That's good news. Hello Monica."

I was quite irritated with the fact that this woman was sitting in my kitchen as if she owned the place. I don't think I would have felt such irritation if she didn't act like I was intruding. I had only been in the same room with Monica on a handful of occasions. We barely spoke. She wore a pinstriped pencil style skirt, with a white blouse with the top buttons undone conveniently showing just enough of her laced nude bra and cleavage. The bottoms of her Christian Louboutin heels matched that of her lipstick which stained the rim of her glass.

"Hey Emily. You should have seen Steven today. This was quite the accomplishment for him and for the firm. I was proud of him."

"I'm always proud of Steven."

Steven could sense the tension. He handed me Lulu, grabbed Monica's glass, and rinsed it out in the sink. The lipstick still lingering leaving her mark. He looked at her and indicated he would get our driver to take her home.

After all the traveling, Lulu was exhausted. I went to lay her down in the nursery and as I came out front, I could see Steven opening the door for Monica to leave. They shared a moment and a brief whisper, and he put his hand on the small of her back as she walked out the door.

I took a deep breath and approached Steven. "Steven, what in God's name would make you think it would be appropriate to have another woman in our home when I'm not here?"

Steven grimaced at my reaction.

"Em, you're overreacting. I have known Monica since high school."

What Steven didn't know is that his mother had slipped one evening and conveyed to me that Monica and Steven were an item in high school and that he only broke up with her to go to Ohio State. Steven's mother didn't care much for Monica. In her words she felt Monica was a gold digger. She conveyed to me that one night, while looking out the window, she saw them by the maze having sex. She was stunned and disgusted by the fact that this girl spread her legs so easily. She indicated that was the only thing she liked about his decision to go to college away from home. In her words," He took out the trash." It made her skin crawl to see he had hired her to work alongside him at the firm and she had warned me to keep my eyes on her. "That girl is not one to be trusted Emily." I could hear her voice now as I was standing before Steven.

54

His inability to see how upset this made me hit me in the gut.

"I'm just disappointed. We have been distant for some time now. All those late nights at the office. You must understand this from my perspective." I didn't dare let on that I knew about his past with Monica. That was a card I would save for later.

"Now that his case is over, I can take time off to be with you and Lulu. You have my word that nothing is going on. You know that I have a lot of responsibility at work and there are many people counting on me. It isn't always cohesive to just take a night off, Emily, Jesus!"

Again, I was trying my best not to allow his abrasive reaction to affect my response.

"I understand, but there needs to be more of an effort on your part to be more present at home. If you could make the time to be home more often, it could help. We both need it."

For the next month Steven was home. In the beginning I could sense restlessness within him. His mind seemed to wander elsewhere and on occasion when I was talking with him, I could tell he wasn't interested, but then he would snap back into reality. I could slowly see him coming back to us once the daily routine kicked in. We were coparenting and when we put Lulu to bed, we focused on us. It felt like we were in back in our apartment in Columbus. We played Scrabble and drank wine. Except for an occasional phone call, there was no law for Steven and no writing for me. It was long overdue.

Submerged

Although it was hard, one night I allowed Vivian to keep Lulu overnight so that Steven and I could be alone together. It had been quite a while since it was just the two of us together, no work. I ordered cheap take-out and we put up a tent in the back yard with a cozy air mattress. We surrounded it with light up lanterns. We made a bonfire and made love under the stars. The ambiance swept me away into that romantic bliss I remembered when I first met him. His touch reminded me of his gentle soul, and I questioned why I ever doubted him. When he leaned into me, I would close my eyes and inhale the smell of his skin. His organic pheromones aroused me and had me wanting more until we fell asleep into each other's arms.

It wasn't until we enrolled Lulu in pre-school that I really started to notice the dramatic increase in my drinking. For Christ's sake I knew the liquor store cashier by name. Susan. I went out of my way into the outskirts of the city every Friday afternoon prior to picking up Lulu from pre-school. I made sure I would get enough for the week. To Susan I had to have been a breath of fresh air to brighten her week. I mean, I had my shit together. A successful novelist married to a very prominent lawyer. I donned my Birkin Bag and drove an Infiniti QX80. The liquor store had a musty cigarette smell and there were always people loitering outside. I'm sure she didn't get very many suburban moms coming in. My visits were becoming more regular, and I didn't want others from the neighborhood seeing me. Then it got to the point where I was hiding my bottles around the house. I didn't want Steven to see that I was becoming unhinged. It was bad enough that he was having an affair. I didn't need to give him ammunition for a divorce. By now I was sure that Steven and Monica were an item. I was a fool and I loved him and denied those lingering feelings. I didn't want to live without him, and I had hoped that there was a chance my intuitions were wrong. That is until Lulu said something to me that annihilated that chance.

A couple of years after I had Lulu, I proposed an idea to Steven for me to get an apartment in the city where I could write. Just a simple one bedroom. It was about twenty minutes away from home and it had a balcony overlooking Boston Harbor. There were times where it was difficult for me to disassociate and create new characters when I was writing from home. I needed a space that would allow me to focus on my writing and inspire me. He agreed and in fact, was all too thrilled. I didn't think much of his excitement until one night after returning home from the apartment and as I was tucking Lulu into bed, she told me about the pretty lady she saw in daddy's bedroom. She said she looked like a princess with blonde hair. Lulu was only three and at the time I thought she was mistaken. Of course, I could be in denial. *He would never bring another woman into our home, would he? Especially with our daughter in the house.*

I thought about confronting him about what Lulu said, but again, I didn't like confrontation, and Lulu was so young, how could I base an accusation like that on what she saw. I pushed it back and clouded those thoughts with more alcohol until I decided to execute a plan to catch him in the act. On a Wednesday afternoon I called Steven at the office and told him in advance that I was going to need to head to the apartment that weekend. I expressed that Gary had pushed up a few deadlines and I needed the time and space to focus. This gave him ample time to adjust his schedule for the weekend and make plans with Lulu. This was when he would typically bond with her and have daddy/daughter time. What Steven didn't know is that I had planned to stake out our home to see if any visitors were to come by while I was away. Friday arrived and I left for the apartment. Tonight, I wasn't going to drink. I wanted to be alert and aware of what was going on as I sat and spied on my family. I pulled up just across the street and parked facing our home and turned the lights to the car off. My stomach was spinning, and I felt like my heart was going to bang out of my chest from the rush of anxiety. It was around 10:00 PM. I knew on Friday nights when I wasn't home that Steven tucked Lulu in around this time. He let her stay up later than usual when it was just the two of them. I figured, if Monica was going to sneak in, then it would be after Lulu was tucked away and asleep. *What was I going to do when I saw her? What was this going to accomplish, and would I leave him after catching him in the act?* I started to feel silly. *What are you doing Emily? Don't you have any trust in your marriage? You're behaving like a child.* I started to allow my inner voices to psych me out of leaving, and just as I was about to head out, I saw her. She pulled up to the gate and pressed the buzzer. I saw the gates open, and she pulled her car into the roundabout driveway. I got out of my car and crept up to the gate obscured by the bushes. I watched as she

58

strutted to the front door. She had a file in hand. Steven opened the door. They spoke for a moment, and she handed him the folder. He leaned in and kissed her on the cheek, and she was back in her car. I ducked as she drove by.

I didn't know what to make of this transaction. She didn't stay but he kissed her. This didn't settle right with me, but once again I denied my intuition and from that night decided to push those thoughts to the side. I couldn't waste any more time focusing on this. If Steven wants to be with her, he will eventually leave me. Until that day comes, I will do what I need to do to stay sane and to remain as attentive as I can to Lulu and being her mom. I decided to go home early the next morning.

When I arrived home the next morning, I heard Steven and Lulu laughing. He was making her favorite blueberry pancakes. She had on her cute duck footed pajamas and her hair was disheveled. She ran to me and hugged me so tight.

"Mommy, you're home early!" she beamed with joy.

"Hi Em. What a nice surprise. Would you like a pancake?" He walked over to me with the spatula in hand and kissed me on the lips. He grinned and I couldn't resist his charm.

"Yes. I would love to have a pancake. Coffee too?"

"Anything for my Em."

Marriage was about compromises. He still loved me, and he still treated me with love, and he took good care of me and Lulu. It wasn't fair of me to make blind accusations. Once again, I make a conscious effort to tuck those thoughts away.

****

The years began to fly by. Lulu was docile but spunky when she needed to be. Her favorite place to visit was the playground at Franklin Park Zoo in the city. She especially enjoyed the tunnel slide. She loved how she could slide down in pure darkness and appear in the sunlight when she got to the bottom. Her arms would stretch out and I would catch her. Her hair was chocolate brown, and she had long curly locks that bounced when she ran. Her green eyes matched Steven's and she was always smiling.

By now Lulu was in school. She was almost six years old and in kindergarten. She had a very vivid imagination and would tell stories for hours. She was extremely friendly, and we had to have discussions with her about stranger danger. I would drop Lulu off in the morning at school and pick her up later in the afternoon. When I wasn't writing, I filled my days with cycling, yoga, and shopping. I often met up with Tonya for lunch and a few drinks. She just had their first child. Her experience as a mom wasn't as pleasant as mine. She often talked about her sleepless nights, and I felt like I was back in the mommy and me group. Of course, it had been almost six years since

Lulu was a baby, so it was hard to connect with her on that level. I always listened and offered my support.

The evenings spent with Lulu were the best. After her bath, we would snuggle up in her bed and I would read to her. Her favorite book was *Mr. Brown can Moo, Can you?* Even though she was getting older she still enjoyed when I would read this to her. It usually was a prequel to another story, but we always started with Dr. Seuss. I loved holding her and being near her. She was my everything. I would lay with her until she fell asleep. Often watching the lights from her carousel night light which rotated and left beautiful images on her walls. She couldn't sleep without it.

Once Lulu fell asleep, I indulged in my wine or on occasion whiskey. I was conscious not to drink around Lulu. I was lonely. I also found myself suffering from anxiety. Those buried thoughts of Steven always had a way of creeping out when the sun went down. We didn't even sleep in the same bed. He stated he got home too late and didn't want to wake me. Our love turned into convenience. He was an amazing dad; but his attempts at being a consistent husband were not up to par. It isn't how I envisioned our marriage to be, and it was a far cry from our college days.

It was early winter, and we had already had our first big winter storm. I had a deadline to meet. Gary was expecting the final chapters of my third novel, and I couldn't find the head space to focus at home. It was the weekend before Lulu's sixth birthday, and I had told Steven

I was going to the apartment for a couple of days to write. I wanted everything sent in so that I could focus on Lulu's birthday party. I had already ordered her an incredibly special gift from Paris, and the guest list was a mile long. I needed things to be right for my perfect girl.

"That sounds good. I have been wanting to take her to the movies to see that new Disney movie. We'll have a good time."

It was a Friday and I decided to leave after dropping Lulu off at school. I gave her a big hug and kiss and told her I would see her in a few days. She looked back at me and gave me one of her Lulu smiles and we waved and blew kisses.

I stopped at the grocery store and of course paid Susan a visit at the liquor store. I always ensured I had all the essentials at the apartment. I didn't want to leave for anything that required driving. Fridays at the apartment were for decompressing. I needed to clear my mind. Emotionally for me, it had been rough at home with Steven.

It was early in the afternoon, and I decided to clean the apartment and light a few candles. I then made a salad, poured a drink, and sat in silence on the balcony with my own thoughts. After a while, when the wine was hitting me exactly right, I turned on some good music and I danced my frustrations away until I was just too tired and passed out.

I was awakened by the sun shining on my face. I could feel my stomach turning. It was sour. I knew immediately that I drank too much the night before. I fell asleep on the couch. The empty wine glass still on the coffee table. In the garbage can the empty wine bottle. I stumbled my way to the coffee pot and started a cup of coffee. I reached for Tylenol and a bottle of water. I knew I was going to need it to meet the deadline.

The phone rang and it was Steven. He wanted to Facetime.

I should say Lulu wanted to Facetime. She usually did whenever I was away.

"Hi Honey. Wow, you look awful. Late night?" Steven snickered.

"Ha, ha. Aren't you the comedian this morning? "I said.

"No, I'm serious. Have you been drinking?"

In the background I could see Lulu.

Before Steven could utter another word, Lulu grabbed the phone.

"Mommy!!! I miss you!"

"There's my beautiful baby girl. Did you sleep well? Mommy misses you already."

"I had the most amazing dream mommy. I was riding a rainbow unicorn. It was so magical! She took me to a faraway land where there was lots of candy and all the animals talked."

It amazed me how much she could articulate her emotions and express herself. She was my special girl and she brought so much joy and happiness into my life. It killed me to be away from her, even though I knew, it was healthy to get away and regroup. I needed to be my best self for her.

"It sounds magical, my little Lulu. I love you more than the moon and the stars. Have fun with daddy. I'll see you very soon."

"Okay, I love you mommy, "and she blew me kisses.

Little did I know that was the last time I would ever see or speak to my daughter ever again.

Chapter 4

Disbelief and Shock

The first stage of grief.

EMILY

The Tylenol kicked in and the shower freshened me up. I was able to dive into the novel I was writing. With everything that had been on my mind the past few weeks, it was hard to focus on what I needed to finish. I was not as far along as I would have liked; however, my outline was thorough, and I knew it was enough of a structure for me to complete it in time. Having a quiet place with no interruptions always helped. I would write with only stopping to use the bathroom or get something to drink. I rarely ate when I wrote. I just needed to focus and put my intent into my work. I typically always met my deadlines; however, my procrastination was getting the best of me. Some weekends I came to the apartment just to get away from Steven. There were days I couldn't stomach being around him. His lies were like tiny knives slowly being inserted into my body one at a time. I needed to numb my spirit and clear my mind of these thoughts as often as I could, and I couldn't be in that state around Lulu.

Before I knew it, the sun went down, and my phone was ringing. I always keep the phone set to the do not disturb setting, but I would allow calls from Steven to come through. I knew Lulu would want to tell me all about her day.

I glanced at the time, and it was just a little past 7:00 PM. *Wow is it really that late?* The time just flew by.

I answered, "Hey, how was the movie? Can I talk to Lulu?"

66

"Emily, I need you to listen very carefully. I need you to stop what you're doing and head to the movie theatre on Front Street."

"What's going on?" Steven very rarely called me Emily. Something didn't seem right.

"It's Lulu. I'll explain when you get here. Please Em, Get here as soon as you can."

"You're scaring me. What's wrong?"

"She's missing."

In that moment I dropped the phone. No... no, this can't be happening. Immediately I grabbed my purse, car keys, threw on my shoes and bolted. I didn't even bother to turn off the lights. It was raining with sleet and hail which turned to a heavy snowfall and the roads were icy. As I drove, a million things were running through my mind. *How could this happen?* I'm sure this is a misunderstanding.

I made a sharp turn into the parking lot where several police cars were parked. Oh God. She really is missing. Just breathe. I'm sure she is fine. You'll walk through that door, and she will be there with Steven, and all will be right in the world.

I stormed through the door to see Steven sitting on the floor with his face cupped in his hands. Beside him was Monica rubbing his back. There were two officers standing on either side of him, one taking notes. Steven stood and grabbed me as soon as he saw me.

"Oh God, Emily. I'm so sorry. I should've brought her myself. I didn't think something like this would happen."

He squeezed me so tight, and I could feel him trembling. I had to compose myself. One of us needed to be calm. This was extremely hard for me to do, especially since I saw Monica sitting. *Why was she here?* I needed to see what was going on. The theatre smell of popcorn and soda resonated, and I started to feel nauseous. I still had no idea what had transpired and how long she had been missing. In that moment I had to put my anxiety, sadness, and bewilderment aside. I needed to focus on the facts and how I could find and bring home my precious baby. I still thought this was a misunderstanding. I just couldn't wrap my head around it.

Once Steven was able to let me go, I asked for answers.

"What do you mean you should've brought her here yourself. Can someone please tell me what is going on? How did this happen?"

"I took her." My eyes darted towards Monica.

She took her! I felt like I was going to explode, and it was taking everything in me to keep my shit together.

"There was an emergency at the firm. Steven needed to go in immediately. A key witness was reconsidering and was on the verge of backing out of his testimony. Lulu was looking forward to going to the movies. I offered to take her. I was going to drop her off at home afterwards." Monica stood just inches from me, smug and completely void of emotion. She was cold and guessing from her demeanor she gave an air that she was in control. This didn't settle right with me.

I could feel my body getting hot and my anxiety was through the roof. I wanted to scream and cry at the same time.

68

"Ma'am, I'm Sargent Black. You can call me Sam." The officer physically inserted his body in between me and Monica.

Monica was lucky the officer interjected. I was clenching my fist and it was taking everything in me not to pummel her face.

"From what I understand your husband's, uhm friend, brought your daughter here. It was crowded. They were in line at the concession stand, and when Monica went to reach for your daughter's hand she wasn't there. We did an extensive search of the theatre, and we currently have officers looking through some of the video footage."

"What? This doesn't make sense. Why would someone take our daughter? Steven, you promised to spend time with our daughter. What the fuck is wrong with you? You are so incompetent. Our child is missing, and this is on you. Do you fucking hear me- on YOU!"

I was falling apart. *Keep it together Em- just keep it together.*

MONICA

I could barely stomach the sight of Emily as she stormed through the door acting as though she was so concerned that her precious daughter went missing. If she was half the mother, she thought she was, she wouldn't be off in her little apartment getting wasted. And here I was playing the part of the doting lover. How could someone be so oblivious as to what has been going on right under her nose? Almost six years I had played the part. I had my sites set on the prize from the day Steven interviewed me, but that isn't where it began.

I met Steven in high school. It was my senior year, and I was the new girl in school. The worst time to start a new school. We came from new money. My father won the lottery, and we went from being low end middle class to having more money than knowing what to do with. It was nothing to be proud of. No matter how much money you give someone, they will never change their ways. My dad was a compulsive gambler hell bent on changing his ways now that he had this newfound money. He decided he had the opportunity to make investments and become a "businessman." He moved us to a suburb of Boston full of influential people and old money. We still ate spam with fried potatoes and onions for dinner while our neighbors were sipping champagne and eating caviar. I might as well have had a target on my back. I didn't fit in. That is until I met Steven.

Submerged

It wasn't hard to tell that I came from new money. This was evident on my first day of school. My clothes said it all. They were that of a K-mart shopper. "Blue light special." It wasn't like you could give me an infusion of "style" overnight. It surely caught the attention of the popular girls who were scantily clad in Chanel and Ralph Lauren and donning their pearls and Gucci bags. I was always the topic of conversation and the inspiration of their snarky jokes. They could try to knock me down, and did they ever try, but at the end of the day, the one thing they could not take away from me was my beauty and they knew it. Boys didn't care about the latest fashion or how much your handbag was. The boys wanted tits and ass. Period. Of course, it was my beauty that turned Steven's head, but beyond that he knew how intelligent and sensitive I was underneath my coat of armor. It didn't matter that the girls called me trash. Steven was the most sought-after boy in school. He came from the most influential family in town, and he wanted me. Not them.

It was my eighteenth birthday and we had been talking for a few months now. He had asked if he could take me shopping. Of course, I couldn't say no. He introduced me to all the upper-class stores and helped me pick out clothes that would help me fit in. That sure shut the other girls up. The next day, I arrived at school, on Steven's arm with more style than any of them had in their pinky finger. He was my Knight in Shining Armor. I was immediately drawn to him and his kindness. He didn't care where I came from. Turns out he lived just three houses down from us. His home was the

71

biggest in town. More of a castle than a house. It looked like something out of a British home magazine. Complete with English gardens and a maze. It was spectacular. We didn't do the normal teenage couple things like attend parties or football games. We volunteered on the weekends at a soup kitchen in the city to help feed the poor and we did whatever we could to give back to others. We met every day after school at his house to study. Grades were important to Steven, and he ensured I didn't fall behind either. Of course, studying isn't all we did during the week. I can't tell you how many times we laid naked under the stars, stroking each other as he licked my supple nipples slowly then sliding his tongue down my inner thighs and then to the parts that made me shiver in pure ecstasy. With each touch my breath got heavier and heavier. Late at night I would sneak outside, and we would meet by the maze. I would strip naked and let him stare as I glided my hands slowly across my breasts and down to my clit where I longed for him to touch me. I would touch it as he watched. I was a teaser, and I loved making him wait. Then I would run. We would get lost in the maze. It was the chase; it was the waiting that made us hot. When he found me, we were like rabbits. We couldn't get enough of each other, and I loved every second of it. It was easy getting Steven to be mine. He loved being inside of me and touching me. I would talk about our future, and I believed with every ounce of my being that we would be married, and I would live in luxury for the rest of my life. I would never want anything if I had Steven forever. My world felt complete.

Submerged

One day after school I went to Steven's house. Their butler let me in, and I waited patiently in the foyer for him. I stood there for some time before I started to wander the halls. The history of this house was impressive. Old photos lined the walls of generations past. It was impeccably clean. There were fresh flowers everywhere and you could smell their fragrant scents mixed with the scent of mahogany and wood polish. I could see myself here, married to Steven and chasing our babies down the hallway. I knew one day this would be mine and our family portrait would hang among the others. I heard muffled yelling and it was coming from Steven's father's study. I could overhear Steven and his father arguing about school. I was surprised to hear Steven say he wasn't going to attend Harvard and that he had plans to go to Ohio. He wanted to go away where people didn't know him. I couldn't believe what I was hearing. Steven's father shouted a rebuttal indicating if Steven did not go to Harvard and get his law degree that he would be disowned and not receive one penny from the estate. I was in a state of shock and backed out of the hall slowly and ran out the front door. I ran home as fast as I could. *How could he do this to me, to us? I thought we would make a life together. The plan was Harvard then he would take over the family firm. We would marry and I would live happily here as his wife. There was never a mention of Ohio.*

I knew at that moment something had to be done to keep him here. An hour or so went by and I could hear my mother letting him in. He gently knocked on my bedroom door.

73

"Hey, you didn't come by today. Is everything okay?"

"Yeah, I'm good. My mom had things for me to do. I was going to call."

I lied. I didn't want him to know that I had overheard his conversation with his father. He owed it to me to tell me himself.

"It's good to see you." I could tell he was not having a good day and that he seemed bothered. Not by me, but by the argument that he had with his father. He looked like he needed a release.

He leaned in slowly pushing me back. He was on top of me, and he started kissing my neck. Instinct took over and I started caressing him and touching him. We peeled off our clothes until our naked bodies were rubbing against each other. I didn't care that we were in my room and my mother was right downstairs, that made us want to do it more. I was being naughty, and Steven liked naughty Monica. I was going to get him so swept up in my trance that he wouldn't even think about the condom. I knew he was in an emotional state. It had to be fast. I gently rolled him over, so I was on top. I loved being in control. I slowly slid it in and pumped and glided as my breasts bounced. I leaned down to kiss him hard, and as I did, I felt the rush of his orgasmic pleasure gush inside of me. His pleasure made me cum, and it was the most amazing feeling I had ever had. It didn't even dawn on him that we were unprotected.

Six weeks later I was pregnant. Steven still hadn't mentioned Ohio by this point, and I wasn't going to let him know that I knew.

74

After all, if he did then he would know this pregnancy was a set-up. I knew once he found out we were expecting that he would have no choice but to attend Harvard and eventually marry me. I wasn't going to let him go.

One night after making love in the gardens, I leaned in. I put my head on his chest. His arms wrapped around me tight. It had cooled down quite a bit and the air smelled of incoming rain. I could feel his chest move up and down as he breathed. I inhaled the scent of his sweet skin and enjoyed the comfort of his arms. This is what it was going to be like. Lying in each other's arms every night embracing one another and loving one another. Perfection.

I whispered, "I'm pregnant."

Silence. Dead Silence.

His breathing was no longer slow and relaxed. It began to feel labored.

"Did you hear what I said?"

"You've got to be kidding, right? There must be some mistake?" He slowly sat up pushing me aside. "Did you see a doctor yet? Maybe the test was wrong."

"I took two tests. Both were positive. I thought you would be happy."

It started to rain. We quickly got up and grabbed our clothes. While getting dressed he said, "What in God's name would make you

75

think I would be happy? I had no intention of staying here in Boston. I had plans. Did you think this was going to last forever? Did you think we would be fucking in the gardens for the rest of our lives? Give me a break Monica. Go home." The rain turned into a torrential downpour and the raindrops stung my skin and hurt just as much as Steven's words.

He turned and walked away. He left me there, in the rain. Sobbing, heartbroken. I certainly didn't think he would be overcome with joy, but his words were harsh. I wasn't expecting to be rejected. Not of this magnitude.

I didn't hear from Steven for a week. Every time I tried calling his mother said he was out. He ignored me at school and didn't walk me to class as he usually did. Others noticed and asked what was going on. I just replied that we were taking a break. I didn't say a word about the baby. Only Steven and I knew, and for now, it would stay that way. Finally, he came by. I was sitting outside on the front porch.

"Hey, do you have a minute to talk?" he said. He looked distant and didn't look like the Steven I knew.

"All I have is time anymore. I was hoping you would come over. Listen I…."

He cut me off… "Look Monica, I am going to make this quick. I am not ready to be a father. I'm only nineteen. I can't tell you what to do with your body, and if you choose to keep this baby, I will support you and send you whatever you need financially for the baby, but this isn't going to work out. I do not want to be a dad. I'm not ready for a family and I don't love you in that way. I have plans to attend Ohio State. I need to get away and make my own choices. I refuse to go to a college where I would be living in my father's shadow." He was visibly shaking. I had never seen him like this. It hurt me to see him this way, but it hurt me more that he was once again rejecting me.

"Take me with you. I'll move to Ohio." I hated the thought of going to Ohio and giving up on all that wealth that could be provided to us. After all, that was my intent on getting pregnant. However, I was convinced that he would eventually see things my way and return home.

"We can make this work. It's our baby Steven. Ours. That says something, doesn't it?"

"No, it doesn't! I'm sorry but this isn't going to work for me. I have plans and you weren't a part of them."

In that moment I saw red. My body had this overwhelming feeling of anger and frustration. Before he could walk away, I yelled, "I'm going to tell your family. How dare you do this to me? Who the fuck do you think you are?" This was no longer about the baby. He never had any inclination to be with me after high school. "You owe me, Steven Van Aken. Do you hear me? You will pay me, and this baby will never want for anything. You are stuck with me forever. "

He grabbed my wrist, and, at that moment, I was scared. I had never seen him lose his temper like this. His eyes pierced right through me.

"If you choose to keep his baby, I will tell my family and trust me, you will not be supported in any capacity. That money would be put into a trust that only he or she will have access to, but only when they are eighteen. That baby will also never carry the Van Aken name. Did you forget sweet Monica that my family owned a law firm. Bring it on." With those last words he turned and walked away.

****

It would be years later when I would see Steven again. I ended up having a miscarriage. Nature had a way of taking care of my sin. Our parents never knew of baby Van Aken. It was a secret that he and I shared even if he hadn't spoken to me in all these years. I went on to graduating high school with honors and went to law school. It only took a few years before my parents ended up going bankrupt but not before they put money into a trust for my education. I was thankful for that. My dad just couldn't stay away from the casinos and eventually he lost all of what was left outside of my trust.

I reconnected with Steven when he returned home from school when his father passed away. At the time he was in a longstanding relationship with Emily. She had no idea who I was, but I watched her with Steven at the funeral. I stalked them with my eyes. She seemed boring and dreadfully dull. Good 'old Steven going for the underdog. I could tell she didn't come from much. I soon realized it wasn't difficult to seduce my long-lost love. He was in my bed as soon as she boarded the plane to go back home. As soon as he saw me and our eyes connected, I felt our sexual tension rise. Immediately I was taken back to the gardens and the cool nights in the maze running naked. I knew he felt it too. I suppose I should've felt guilty for fucking his brains out when he was taken; however, he was mine first. I was meant to be with him and embrace the luxury of his family money. It nearly broke me when he left to go to Ohio State. *Who turns down an Ivy League school to move to Ohio?* I was infatuated with Steven, and I loved him in high school. Our chemistry was undeniable. Our life was meant to be spent together and his leaving ruined that for me.

That night together was full of lust; and he was still the best fuck I ever had.

After Steven went back to school, I met David. He wasn't financially stable like Steven, but he was a daredevil. Everything about him screamed spontaneity. He enjoyed taking risks and I felt my adrenaline rush each time I was with him. He made me feel exhilarated with every moment we spent together. In time just seeing him made me wet. He was a man not a boy. He didn't come from much and he was always looking for an opportunity. He wasn't very successful at work, and he was reckless with money. We were both broke. I had money left in my trust, but I made a promise to myself that it would pay for the remainder of law school. I knew once I graduated with my law degree that I could build an empire all my own and become a successful lawyer. Our relationship was off and on. David was unstable and at times I questioned what his intentions were with me. I knew he was seeing other women, but it didn't bother me too much as I was focused on my future and on occasion had a few one-night stands of my own.

After getting my law degree and becoming a lawyer, I was contacted by a headhunter who indicated that Steven Van Aken of the Van Aken law firm wanted to interview me for a possible position. I had busted my ass to be at the top of my class in school and I was now starting to make a name for myself within the city as one of the top female lawyers around. I was becoming more financially stable, but this could put me at the top. While I despised Steven for what he did to me years ago, I still had feelings for him. He was after all my first love, and he took care of me when no one else did. He helped me to become the lawyer I am today by pushing me to be my best in school. I hesitated, but I took the interview, and less than a week later I was offered the position. Of course, he was now married to Emily, and they were already expecting their first child. I was bitter. That could have been me, and I knew that at any moment if I wanted to, I could sweep the rug right out from underneath Emily's feet, and she wouldn't even see it coming. Of course, after accepting the position David started coming around more often and admitted his feelings for me and that he had been an idiot. He made a full commitment to me, and David loved me. He understood my ambitions and my desires, but he also knew of my past and my connections. The most important connection was that

Submerged

I once dated the son of the most influential man in Boston and all I had to do was shake my ass to get his attention. He was always scheming and plotting his next move to make money and there wasn't anything I wouldn't do for David. Now that I was working with Steven, David saw opportunity knocking on his door and together we knew that I could seek revenge on Steven for what he did to me all those years ago and we could walk away with more money than we would ever know what to do with. It would take time, and it would take perseverance.

STEVEN

Lulu hung up the phone with Emily before I could say goodbye. I was relieved she was away for the weekend. Things just weren't the same. I noticed a change in Emily. Her drinking was starting to get out of control, and she was making more visits to the apartment. I was starting to get concerned that her drinking would carry over into the days while I was at work, and she was with Lulu. I know I haven't been the most attentive husband but Jesus she had everything she needed. She was taken care of. I loved Emily but I just couldn't get past this change in her. It was as if all her ambitions were gone; even her writing was starting to suffer. She was procrastinating and I happened to see an e-mail from her agent one day when she left her laptop open, indicating that she was missing deadlines. I found this odd since she was spending more time at her apartment in the city. Before Lulu, writing was her passion. I remember her spouting ideas and constantly jotting down lines and phrases in her journal that she carried everywhere. Her characters took on a life all their own and I was intrigued with her ability to create such fantasies. I loved watching her when she wrote. It was as if everyone and everything around her was gone and it was just her in her own little bubble. A freight train could whiz right by, and it wouldn't faze her. Her creative nature was such an attraction to me, and now that seemed to dissipate.

We were winning cases left and right at the firm. We were successful, and I found pure pleasure in this success, but the cases were piling up and it had been more stressful than ever. I needed

82

something to alleviate that stress and take my mind off the mundane duties of life in general.

Hiring Monica at the firm turned out to be one of the best business decisions I made. Clients came from all over wanting her representation. We made a good team. My workdays turned into late evenings and before I knew it, I was falling for Monica. She was different from when I knew her in high school. She changed. She wasn't this obsessive, desperate, middle-class girl with a high school crush anymore. Monica's drive at the firm and her need to be in charge was extremely attractive to me. She didn't have a care in the world and certainly took control of cases when needed. She never wavered in her thoughts. She had such independence, and the world was in the palm of her hands. It was hers for the taking. I envied that freedom.

Lulu was the light of my life. I adored her sweet nature and curiosity. Spunky and independent yet creative and carefree. I couldn't wait to spend the afternoon with her. I promised her a movie with popcorn and junior mints. I always looked forward to our days together. My father always put work before family, and I didn't get that time with him. I wanted to make sure I was present in Lulu's life and made a conscious effort to let her know how much she was loved. I never thought I could love another human being as much as I loved my Lulu. It didn't matter to me what was going on between me and Em. She gave me the greatest gift, my baby girl.

Submerged

On the way to the movies, I had to stop at the office in the city to pick up some paperwork. I tried to avoid work on the weekends, especially when I had time with Lulu, but one of our biggest cases was scheduled to start on Monday and some loose ends needed to get taken care of. I knew Monica would be over when I put Lulu to bed, and we could get some work done. It wasn't unusual for Monica to spend the night on the weekends when Emily was at her apartment. I often snuck her in after Lulu was in bed and she would be gone by the time she woke in the morning. It wasn't like I was fucking her in Emily's bed. I had my own room. Either way it didn't matter. I wanted Monica and I enjoyed my time with her. Besides, Emily was too interested in her late-night drinks to even notice I had been having an affair and Monica and I had an arrangement.

As we neared the office building, we passed Emily's apartment. Lulu pointed and said, "Look Daddy Mommy's work." I wondered if she was writing or just passed out on her couch.

We arrived at the office and Stan, the front desk security officer welcomed us and gave Lulu a sucker. Her favorite flavor, cotton candy. Lulu ran to the elevator. Her favorite part was pressing all the buttons; however, I had to tell her today only push the button for daddy's floor. We need to get to the movies. She giggled and said, "okay daddy." She looked up at me with her sweet smile and her glistening green eyes. The office was empty, except I knew Monica would be in. She was dedicated to her work. Sure enough, I rounded the corner and saw her in her office on the phone. She had a look of concern on her face. As I approached her, she held up her hand as if to tell me not to speak. Her calm nature starts to rise to panic, and this was unusual for her. Her next words to the mysterious caller indicated to me we had a big issue.

"Hold on for one moment. Steven just walked in. Let me fill him in and I'll have him call you back within the hour. Hang tight." Monica hung up the phone, stood up from her desk and stated, "We have a big problem."

Lulu shouted, "Hi Monica!"

"Hi Sweetie. "Monica turned to me and indicated our key witness in Monday's trial was getting cold feet and wanted to back out of testifying, He was the key to this case and without him we had a slim to no chance of winning.

"Someone has spooked him. He received threats last night against his family."

"How in the hell did this happen? We have been cautious about his anonymity. You and I were the only people that knew of his willingness to testify. We have been clear about not telling anyone. He is our key witness."

"Well, he has no intentions at this point of testifying unless we can offer him and his family full protection."

I grabbed Monica and pulled her into the hall. Leaving Lulu spinning in Monica's office chair.

'Fuck! What the hell Monica. I need to get a hold of Brian and Mike and see what we can do here. I don't think we can just get protection without cause. Not only that, but it's also Saturday. I'm going to need to call in some favors."

"Daddy, daddy, are we going to the movies now?"

Shit. It was my day with Lulu. She was really looking forward to this. Monica could sense my concern.

"Look, I know you promised to take Lulu today. Why don't you let me take her? When the movie is over, I can meet you back at your place. I'll grab a pizza and we can eat together at the house. She will be fine."

"Are you sure? I mean I know it isn't ideal, but we can't let anything disrupt this case."

Monica smiled and whispered. "I got this. How hard could it be. Besides, I haven't been to the movies in ages. "

"Lulu, how about if I take you to the movies today and we can meet your daddy later and have pizza!" Monica tried to make it sound appealing, but I could see the disappointment in Lulu's eyes.

I knelt to Lulu's level and gave her a tight squeeze. "Lulu, honey, daddy has a work emergency. I am so sorry. I promise to make it up to you." I kissed her softly on the forehead. It broke me to give up this day.

Lulu hugged me back and nodded her head. "I'll have pizza with you later." She kissed my cheek and grabbed Monica's hand. "Let's go Monica. We're going to be late."

I watched as Monica walked down the hall with my heart and immediately got on the phone. This was going to be a long day and I had to ensure my witness and his family were protected and that I made it home in time to meet the promise I made to my Lulu.

****

Luckily, I was able to secure my witness and his family in a discreet location with a guard. I headed back to the house eager to see my girls. It wasn't long after that my phone rang, and Monica was on the other end hysterical.

"Monica, calm down. What is wrong?"

In between her sobs, Monica made me promise not to get upset with her. I made the promise only on the premise of her calming down. I needed to know what was going on.

"Steven, I lost Lulu. I lost her."

'Monica where are you? Tell me where you are. I am coming to you."

"I'm at the movie theatre. The police are here. She is gone Steven. Gone."

In that moment I froze. It took a moment to register what she said. I immediately turned the car around and headed to the theatre.

****

When I arrived, Monica was sitting on a bench near the concession stand. Two to three officers surrounded her. She saw me and immediately jumped up and ran to me.

"Steven, I'm so sorry. We were in line, and she was right there. When I turned to grab her hand, she was gone. I looked everywhere. You know how she can be. She is so curious, and she was upset that you didn't come along. She complained the entire ride here."

I tried to ignore the fact that she blamed this on my Lulu. She was only five years old and a child. However, I understood the fact that she was upset and not thinking clearly. I considered calling Emily, but I didn't want to put her in a state of panic. I was still in denial and hoping that Lulu was just hiding somewhere. I was sure she was still here, and we could take her home.

An officer approached me, "Mr. Van Aken? I'm Officer Black. We have scoured the theatre and there is no sign of your daughter. We have cause to believe she was taken. Now we had some officers looking through the video feed and the last sighting of her was near the door, but she stepped out of sight of the video. We currently have officers in the office searching for other angles in hopes of getting a glimpse of what happened. Your wife states she was at the concessions stand when she turned, and your daughter was no longer there. The manager confirmed that the theatre was exceptionally busy tonight due to the anticipation of this movie."

"She is not my wife."

"Excuse me?" Officer Black looked confused. "My apologies, she never indicated otherwise."

"I need to call her mother, my wife. What am I going to say?" I started to fill with panic, and it felt as if my legs were going to give out beneath me. I reached for the wall and slowly lowered myself to the ground. This wasn't happening. This can't be happening.

"Mr. Van Aken. We are doing everything we can. Try to collect yourself then I would encourage you to make that phone call."

I looked at my cell phone, hesitated, then called Emily. She is never going to forgive me for this. Never.

MONICA

I reveled in the fact that Emily was losing her shit and I quietly stepped back as she threw her tantrums at Steven. I asked one of the officers if I could use the restroom. I quietly exited the commotion and entered the bathroom checking every stall to ensure I was alone. I immediately called David. He didn't answer right away, it took a few rings, but when he did it sounded like he had been running.

"David, what's going on, can you hear me?" He was breathing heavily, and he didn't speak right away. I could hear the wind howling through the phone. "Where are you?"

"Monica? Can you hear me? Monica?"

The phone went dead.

Fuck!

Holy Fuck.

Something's wrong. I needed to get out of here.

Chapter 5

Denial

The second stage of grief.

EMILY

Eventually the officers suggested that we all head home and if anything, transpires they would let us know. *Is this how it worked? We just sit and wait?* Steven had his back to me, but I saw Monica whispering in his ear as she glanced over at me. She kissed him on the cheek and smirked before heading to her car. I wanted to kill her. I couldn't believe the audacity.

I didn't know how I could drive myself home. *Do I go home, or do I go to my apartment?* The tension between Steven and myself was more than I could bear. I wanted to break down that barrier and have him wrap his arms around me. I needed him.

Steven turned and our eyes met. I could see his pain. I knew he could see mine. We were broken.

He came to me and held out his arms. I let him embrace me and we both stood there in silence. It felt like minutes before he offered to drive me home. To our home together.

"Are you sure you don't want me to go to the apartment?" It wasn't until now when I realized he no longer felt for me the way that he used to. I could see it in his eyes. I could sense it in his touch. We were untethered and my eyes were open. I didn't deny his affair and I knew he was no longer mine.

"I can have someone pick up your car. I don't want you driving in this condition and alone. We have talking to do, but right now is not the time. Our only focus should be Lulu and we should be together to support the process while they search for her."

I agreed. Lulu was the number one priority. He gently ran his hand down my arm, as he looked away, and we walked to the car.

There were two officers that followed us home. They indicated due to Steven's status within the community that FBI agents would be arriving as this could potentially be a ransom kidnapping. They wanted to have a presence near us in case anyone reached out to us.

We arrived at the house, and it was dark. Sadness was looming. I was numb and I wanted to get back in the car and drive. Scour the neighborhood and knock on every door, but I was emotionally drained. I changed my clothes and headed straight for the liquor cabinet. I needed something strong, and this was the first time, other than casual dinners, when I poured a drink in front of Steven. He obviously had no qualms over hiding his affair and I no longer cared that he saw me drink. I knew he was aware of my drinking, but it was easy to pretend he didn't know if he didn't see me. I grabbed the Jack and some coke. First, I downed a shot, straight up. Then I made my drink, grabbed the whiskey and my glass, and headed towards Lulu's room.

I had every intention of sitting in her bed and inhaling the smell of her from her pillow but as soon as I entered the doorway I broke down. I couldn't bear to go into her room. Not like this. Not now. I wanted to leave it untouched until she came home. I went back downstairs and sat on the sectional. I didn't turn on any lights, I sat in pure darkness, crying, trembling. I could see Steven's silhouette in the doorway. He didn't speak. He just stood there watching me. I had hoped he would have come to me. We could have comforted each other. Perhaps I would have let up on the drinking if I had some other form of comfort, but instead he turned and went to his room. I thought about calling my mom and Tonya, but I had hoped Lulu would come through the front door with one of the officers, safe.

MONICA

David and I had elaborated a plan and I feared something had
gone wrong. We had rented an efficiency suite under aliases in a seedy
neighborhood. I sped there as fast as I could. I pulled in and moments
later David appeared. He looked pale, wet, and cold. No Lulu. We
hurried inside and I turned to face him.

"What the fuck David. Where is Lulu? You were supposed to
bring her here."

"Monica you're not supposed to be here. What if someone saw
you? There is a change in plans. I took her to my sister's place. She is
out of town and her house is in a more rural area outside of the city."
He started to undress. I could tell he was distracted.

"David, I panicked. You didn't sound right on the phone. Why
didn't you mention her place?" We had gone over the plan a million
times. It had to be seamless.

"After thinking about it my gut just told me that this wasn't a
great location. I was afraid that someone might hear her or see her
here. I tried to tell you earlier, but I lost service, and the phones were
disconnected. The kid can't see you. I was going to call you once I got
out of these wet clothes."

I was furious that he steered away from the course, and it was
not sitting right with me, but this was David. Spontaneous and

95

indecisive. I had to accept the change and hope that this played out the way it needed to. If this worked, we would be set for life and were free to do anything we wanted to. Over five years of this. Plotting and planning and saving my own money. I was ready to disappear.

"Is she ok? Did you leave her food and water? Why are you all wet?"

"Monica, relax! Why all the questions? She isn't a dog. In case you haven't noticed it is wet outside. I need to think of our next step. The ransom call. We can't fuck this up." His agitation was sexy. He leaned into me, and I placed my hands on his bare chest. Damn he looked good.

He was right. I needed to focus and keep my mind clear. We were almost there.

"You're right. I am panicking. Just promise me you will go back tonight to stay with her. She is just a pawn so we can get our money. I don't want anything happening to her." I had no emotional attachment to Lulu. I just didn't want murder added to the list of charges if we were to be caught.

David looked at me dumbfounded and the look in his eyes was something I had never seen before. I blew it off thinking it was just the adrenaline and the rush of everything that was happening.

"Monica we can have no contact with each other until after the drop. Do you understand me?"

I nodded slowly and stared at him. He looked vulnerable at that moment, and I wanted him. The thought of having everything we ever wanted and having him with me made me feel almost euphoric. I was addicted to this man. We were both wet from the snow and cold. In that moment I took him in. All of him. He didn't even bother to fully undress me. He turned me around and bent me over the small table that was in the center of the efficiency suite, and he took all of me. It was hard, it was sensual, it was what I needed in that moment. I could hear the people above us fucking. It was loud and she let out endless screams and moans. I loved it. I looked up at the ceiling wishing I could see them, and I leaned up while he was still in me and pulled my shirt off. He grabbed my breasts and squeezed. I was ready to climax, but I didn't want this to end so I held it in until I knew he was ready. I reached down and rubbed my wet pussy and in that moment we both came.

I knew I wouldn't see David until after we picked up the ransom. I wanted to be with him longer before he left to babysit. We laid for hours naked waking from our slumbers to fuck some more and then he left to go to his sister's place. From there we would cut off any communications until the day of the drop. I was to go about my daily routine as usual and keep ties with Steven. My instructions were to stay connected with Steven as I have always done and inquire about Lulu. I was to seem concerned and offer solace. Steven was in love with me. Just a week ago he told me he was leaving Emily and wanted to start a life together. This was the perfect time to arrange the kidnapping.

The plan for the next five days was for David to stay with Lulu and then make the ransom call. I would grab the money from the drop off location while David dropped Lulu off at Franklin Park. David would then meet me with the new passport and our bags packed and we would drive to the airport together. By then Lulu would be back home and we would be long gone.

Submerged

EMILY

Three days had passed. I stayed on the sofa only getting up to use the bathroom and refill my glass. The only calls we received from the police were to tell us that there were no updates. Steven was out every day. Searching, asking questions. He was at the theater everyday trying to revive the events that transpired that day. He hired a private investigator the night Lulu went missing and there was a search team out looking for her. We spoke to the media and were featured on the evening news. Anything we could do to bring her home. Time was crucial, every hour that passed put her farther away from us. We had agents at the house, but they insisted that I stay home in case anyone called the land line. By this time, Steven had called my mom and she and Terry were with us. She couldn't believe the state I was in.

"Em, I'm here. Mom is here for you." She hugged me and for a moment I didn't want her to let go. I just wanted to break down in tears, but I didn't deserve this kindness. This was my fault. If I hadn't put things off and spent my weekends drinking and drowning in the fear of Steven's infidelity, then I would've been home that day. I could've taken my sweet baby to the movies.

Tonya was with me as much as she could be, and Jacob never left Steven's side. Steven's mom and sister were only minutes away so they were searching and at the house as much as they could be. We were waiting anxiously for a ransom letter, call, anything that could help us to understand why someone would take her. Then it happened. We received the call.

It was 8:00 AM on day four. It was early. I was hungover. My mom was trying to get me to eat, but I couldn't. Our home phone never rang except for the occasional telemarketer, so it startled me. The agent was to signal me when I could answer so that he could track the call and record the communication. He gave me the thumbs up, and I answered.

"Hello?" I was nervous. The agents had run the scenarios with me a thousand times these last few days, but I don't think any amount of preparation could help.

"Mrs. Van Aken, I have your daughter. If you ever want to see her again then you will deliver one million dollars in unmarked bills to the Boston Fish Pier. There is an old, abandoned fishing boat called the Salty Dog. There is a storage bench in the stern of the boat. Leave the money there by midnight tomorrow. Do not involve the police. If you do, then you will never see your daughter again."

The phone clicked. The call ended. I could barely move. The caller disguised their voice using some a voice changing device. *A million dollars?*

I looked at the agent. He didn't have enough time to track the call. I immediately grabbed my cell phone and called Steven.

Steven barely uttered hello, "Come home now. There was a call and there is a ransom. We need to get the money together." With that Steven hung up the phone and within ten minutes he was home.

The FBI agents explained that this could be a ploy, a game. The caller offered no proof of life. It could be anyone. By now news had spread about the disappearance of Lulu. Afterall, we had the entire community out looking for her.

"I don't care. If there is a chance this is the real kidnapper then I'm, we're, not taking any chances!" Steven looked at me and he grabbed my hand. "We will get her back Em."

He looked back at the agents. "We will get her back. Money is no object for us. Whatever they need."

It was early enough in the day, and Steven started calling our banks. It wasn't going to be easy to get that amount of cash within the time frame; however, Steven knew people and I knew he could make it happen. For a fleeting moment I saw a shimmer of light.

Submerged

Chapter 6

Guilt

The third stage of grief.

EMILY

Night crept up on us. Steven had spent the day gathering money for the ransom and calling in favors. Every influential person in Boston was under his command to bring our Lulu home. He finally took a moment to rest. I think that he felt confident in Lulu's return. I wasn't so optimistic. I kept replaying what the FBI agents told us. Thoughts raced through my mind. *What if Lulu didn't come home?*

Steven's mom went home with Paige, and I had insisted that mom and Terry go upstairs and lay down. I needed to be alone. I felt as though I hadn't had a moment to breathe without someone hovering over me like a hawk. I grabbed the Jack and a sweater and headed to the porch swing out back. The snow glistened in the moonlight. The air smelled fresh and crisp, but it was cold and harsh. The warmth of the whiskey coated my throat. Drinking, at this point, was the only way I would get any sleep. It numbed me. I inhaled deeply and closed my eyes. I could see Lulu. It was last winter, and she insisted on playing in the snow. I bundled her up in her Burberry snow suit complete with a matching scarf. Her gloves, hat, and boots were red, and I watched as she excitedly dragged her saucer sled up our hill on the far end of the back yard. I sat on our back deck as she insisted, she wanted to go alone. The air was frigid, and the snow was virgin white. Untouched. Lulu's footprints christened it and showed signs of life. I can still hear the crunch, crunch of the snow as she took each step. The snow was so deep and at times she stumbled into it, but she picked herself up, unscathed, and laughing. Once she got to the top of the hill, she settled her saucer and sat Criss cross applesauce in the middle of it.

She yelled, "Mommy, count to three!"

I said it then and I say it now, aloud, "One- Two- Three!"

I see her push herself down the hill as she soars down the snow banked hill screeching and giggling the entire way. My eyes snap open. The only sound that existed was the howl of the wind and the creek from the swing. I took another drink and sobbed. The tears flowed until they froze to my cheek. I'm not sure how long I stayed outside. At some point I must have made my way in the house and onto the couch.

I was awakened by a knock on the door.

The sound of the knock seemed low at first- then proceeded to get louder and louder. I passed out in a drunken stupor. I couldn't move. The past four days of endlessly searching, worrying, and imagining what was happening to my sweet baby girl took their toll on me. At this point I was helpless. I had no control, and I couldn't stand the thoughts that raced through my mind. I looked at the clock and it was a little after 4:00 in the morning.

I could see the reflection of the flashing lights in the front window. I blinked and headed to the door slowly realizing that either they had found her, and she was safe, and I could wrap my arms around her dainty body, or we would get terrifying news. I caught a glimpse of myself in the mirror. My hair knotted, mascara running, and I smelled. I was still drunk, and I felt sick to my stomach. I didn't even realize that Steven and my mom and Terry were behind me. Another knock on the door and I froze. I slowly opened it. I felt like I was in a movie. A horror movie. There stood officer Black looking solemn. His mouth was moving but I didn't want to believe what he was saying. It was as if the air had been sucked out of the room. My vision became tunneled, and I felt myself slowly slipping away.

I woke with the smell of ammonia under my nose and could hear the EMT yell, "she's responsive."

Once my vision cleared, I saw a plump young lady hovering above me. "Miss, how much have you had to drink?"

The officers just told me they found my child's lifeless body in a nearby frozen lake and you're asking me how much I had to drink?

"Fuck Off!" I screamed in her face and tried to stand. I was physically and emotionally unstable. My entire world had fallen apart. My heart ached so badly, and I thought it was going to explode. Steven was there sobbing and reaching for me. He caught me as I fell and screamed.

"My baby... My sweet Lulu," I cried repeatedly. I pounded on Steven's chest until he just grabbed me and hugged me as tight as he could. He wouldn't let me go. I didn't want him to. I wanted him to hug me as tight as he could until he took the breath out of me, and I was with my little girl.

MONICA

It was the fifth day. I hadn't spoken to David since I saw him the night our plan commenced. I missed him and I was anxious to be with him again. I had done my best to get a hold of Steven, but he wouldn't return any of my calls or texts. I needed to make it seem like business as usual. I couldn't let on that I had anything to do with Lulu's disappearance. It was to be expected that I wouldn't have much communication with him. It was better this way. I went to work just as I did every day. I tried to pretend like I was concerned and unaware regarding Lulu. I was leaving tonight. I would never see Steven again.

People may think six years is a long time to successfully execute a plan; however, it had to be the perfect plan. Layered like a cake. Enticement, seduction, longing, trust, and frosted with emotion. Once a man falls in love, they become blind. Blind to the obvious signs of deception. Steven's love for me clouded his judgement. He fell in love, and he fell hard. My persuasions worked and I was able to get close enough to Steven where I was sleeping in his bed and taking his daughter on outings. He trusted me, just as I trusted him years ago, but this time I had the upper hand. I would be lying if I said I didn't develop feelings for him again, but I had to focus on the end game. Nights when I was with him in his bed, wrapped in his arms feeling safe and Lulu sleeping soundly in the next room, I would envision it as it should have been all those years ago. If only he had stayed with me.

Submerged

If only I didn't miscarry. Then I am reminded that he didn't love me. He didn't give a second thought to breaking my heart and now I promised not to doubt my choice to break his. Having love for him when he betrayed me made it easy to deceive him. It was easy to get him to trust me. And he did.

If it were up to David, the kidnapping would have happened much sooner. It took convincing to get him to see the big picture. On occasions when I would come home to David, he would violently inhale my scent and fall into a fit of jealousy stating I smelled like Steven and that we needed to just get it over with already so we could move on. Once, he was so enraged that he threw me against the wall. His whole body pressed against mine as he punched a hole in the wall just inches from my face. I was terrified and shocked. When he saw the bewilderment on my face, he would come to reality. Gently caressing my face and apologizing profusely. He would then make passionate love to me, reminding me over and over that he loved me so much that he just couldn't stand the thought of me with someone else.

Steven often asked about David, and I contemplated telling him of the abuse and just letting this plan end. However, David was the world to me, and I was willing to sacrifice anything for him. I just continued to let Steven know that David was equivalent to Emily. I could leave him when Steven said the word.

That day finally came when Steven approached me in my office. He handed me a folder. Within it were the divorce papers he was going to serve Emily. I was speechless. He talked about this, but I didn't think he was ever going to follow through. Not with Lulu. I knew how much he loved being a father, and he didn't want to ruffle the marriage and have Lulu raised in a broken home. Emily's drinking and drunken escapades made it easier for him to do this now. After looking within the folder, I looked up at him, and said, "is this real? Is this happening?"

"Yes. I had Robert draw up the papers for me last week. It's done. I just need Emily's signature. Here. I also got this for you."

He handed me a blue Tiffany box. Within it was a gold diamond necklace. A notecard was placed with the necklace that stated. *This is a symbol of our new life together. I never should have let you go. Yours forever, Steven.* This was all I wanted since I met him years ago. However, now my path and priorities changed. I was a woman now and I needed a man who could take control and be precise in his emotions. I couldn't afford to be with someone whose feelings waivered at the drop of a dime. It was within this moment I decided now was the time to execute our plan. I got what I wanted, but I no longer wanted it. I wanted David and I wanted a life far from here. Steven would soon forget about me just as he did before, and he would live out his life with his drunk wife and his little girl.

****

My apartment was nearly empty. I lived minimally these past years and had I made no connection to this place and these things. I knew I would be on to bigger and better things. I packed all my essentials and some memorabilia. I was leaving my life here and I would start a new one elsewhere as a new person. I ensured I had the passports. David already set up bank accounts offshore in our new names. I put every ounce of trust into David. We discussed the plan, and we had been prepared. I was confident that everything would go smoothly. By now the ransom call should have been made and David would have given them proof of life. I heard whispering at the office that a ransom call was made; therefore, I didn't question that the plan went off the rails. David was to instruct Emily and Steven to pick Lulu up at the Franklin Park Zoo playground after making the drop. It was my job to grab the money once I saw Steven get in his car and leave. Lulu was never supposed to see me, and I hadn't seen her since David took her from the theater. David would then come to the pier, pick me up on the far end and we would head to the airport.

I was nervous. I knew it would be highly unlikely for Steven to drop off that amount of money and not have the authorities involved. I would be stupid to think that he would put it in the bench of the boat and just leave even if it was to pick up his daughter.

I concocted a plan to retrieve the money. Weeks before we took Lulu and the ransom call had been made, I had paid a visit to the abandoned boat on the pier. I inspected the bench. The one in which Steven was to place the one million dollars. The boat wasn't in the best shape. You could tell that the wood was starting to rot. I was surprised that it was still in the water. At the bottom of the bench there as a

111

panel. A removable panel. Held in place by nuts and bolts. One could easily remove the bolts, making it easy to slide the panel and retrieve whatever was inside the bench from below the boat. Of course, I would have to remove the bolts before the ransom call was made. I would also have to purchase a dry scuba suit and the other gear to sustain being under water. The water temperature this time of year is freezing, and I would need a suit that would keep me insulated and prevent hypothermia.

On one of our adventures together David and I took diving lessons. We took a trip to the Bahamas after David came into some money. He said one of his Business "ventures" paid off. While in the Bahamas we learned how to go diving and use scuba gear. I learned which suits were best for certain temperatures of the water. I was so fascinated with it and immediately fell in love.

One night I went out to the boat with my gear. It was a little past midnight, and it was very dark. Only one light lit up the dock and I could tell it wouldn't be hard to conceal myself under the pier. I went under the water beneath the boat. The way the boat was positioned there was just enough of a gap between the water and the stern. I could get under the boat and easily slide that panel. I would be able to conceal a waterproof duffel under the pier where I could transfer the bag into before going under and swimming to the other side. No one would see me. I would swim to the other side of the harbor and have David pick me up there. Once Steven dropped the bag I would wait then dive below the boat and retrieve the money. If Steven did notify authorities, they would be looking for someone on land. Sounds like a plan made for movies but this was a million dollars, and it was all I needed to get out of this fucking town and live a life I deserved.

STEVEN

I was holding Em up. She could barely stand as the news of Lulu's death came crashing down on all of us. Emily's mom and Terry were there and none of us could speak. We were all in shock. I couldn't cope with the news, neither could Em. I had to be the strong one. I had to be the anchor because I was all that she had.

Emily had fallen apart, and I only had myself to blame for all of this. *What did I do to my family?* I wanted to grieve, and I wanted to give up, but this was on me, and I needed to keep it together. The EMT was tending to her, and they gave her a banana bag. She was unstable and they wanted to take her immediately to the hospital. Em fought them and pleaded with me to let her stay. I told the EMT that she would be fine at home. This was the best place for her and insisted that they monitor her for a bit. I knew this was against regulation but given the circumstances she agreed. I could see the sorrow and the pity in her eyes. She didn't know what she was walking into when police had called the ambulance.

"I'm sorry for what I said Mr. Van Aken. About her drinking. I had no idea."

I touched her hand and told her not to worry and that I appreciated her for looking after Em. I turned to the agents.

"I don't understand. We just received the call early yesterday and we had until midnight tonight. Why would someone ask for money if she was dead?"

"We mentioned this to you previously Mr. Van Aken. We see this all the time. More than likely the ransom call was from someone unaffiliated with your daughter's disappearance and was just trying to embezzle money from you."

Talking to the officers only reiterated how much I fucked this up. I was stunned. I couldn't believe the news that was delivered. The officers stated we needed to go to the morgue to identify the body.

Monica had been texting me all night. I couldn't concern myself with her right now. I loved her but this was my daughter, my family. She was the reason I lost my forever.

****

After time, Emily started to sober up. The banana bag helped and the EMT left. Emily insisted on going to the morgue. I did not believe she was in any condition to view the body. There was a chance this was not Lulu; although, according to the officers, the body had on the exact same clothes that Lulu was wearing the day of her disappearance.

Lulu had this outfit she insisted on wearing that day. When I first saw her in it, I was shocked. It was extremely stylish, and I thought *how does a five-year-old come up with this?* Em and I always encouraged her to go with it and create her own style. She had on sage green and pink camo pants. With it she wore an oversized cashmere sweater that was pink. Her hair was long, shiny, and healthy with thick bouncy curls, and she wore a black snow cap and high-top black Timberland boots. She wore the bracelet that Em and I had gotten for her. It was a 14K rose gold ID style bracelet. It had her monogram on it. On the other side it said, "To our forever Lulu, Love mom and dad." She never took that bracelet off and it fit her like a glove.

Against my better judgement I took Em to the morgue. I wasn't thinking straight. I was reeling from the anticipation and adrenaline of the past few days with the hopes of Lulu coming home and finding out she was gone. Gone forever.

I ached for Em. She was in a state of non-reality. Depressed, but most of all in shock. She was unrecognizable to me. I was not worthy of being her husband. I was not worthy of comforting or protecting her. I had failed her; I had failed our family. If only I had been there for her instead of spending time with someone else, maybe she wouldn't be drunk.

As we waited in the hall for the detective, my phone rang. It was the private investigator I had hired the night Lulu went missing. Salvatore LaCroix.

Salvatore was a highly respectable private investigator. I had known him for years and he helped me with some of our trial cases. When Lulu went missing, he was the first person I called. Once I arrived at the movie theatre that night and saw that the police couldn't locate her, I made the call. I had to divulge in the news of my affair with Monica. Frankly, he didn't seem to be surprised. According to Salvatore those within the firm knew of the affair and eventually he got wind of it. Sal asked about Monica.

"Steven, do you trust Monica?" What kind of question was that. I loved Monica of course I trusted her.

"Steven, are you there?" I felt like I was in limbo, and I was just going through the motions of things. Answering calls, nodding yes or no to questions. I was in a zombie like daze.

"Of course, I trust her. Afterall, I let her take my daughter to the movies." I was adamant that Monica had nothing to do with this. However, in the back of my mind I kept replaying what I had said to Sal. *I let her take my daughter to the movies.*

"Sal, I can't talk now. Em and I are at the morgue." I could barely say the words. I was trying so damn hard to keep it together. I could feel my stomach churning and I was getting lightheaded. I didn't know if I could do this. *Could I identify her body?* I was holding Em up when I could barely stand myself.

"Steven, I heard the news, this is why I am calling. I need you to listen carefully. I have secluded the team that found Lulu's body and I have talked with the lead detective on the case. It is very important that you do not let it leak out that Lulu is dead. Most of all

117

do not tell Monica. I know that sounds impossible and I hate to ask this of you, but this is very crucial."

"Sal, what's going on, do you know something? How can I hide this? I haven't even identified her body yet." I needed to deal with one thing at a time. I took a deep breathe.

"Take this time to be with Emily. I am just asking you to remain silent about Lulu's death. This is very important. I have a lead. I may know who is responsible for this. We need to act quickly. I need you to be strong and focused. I know that will be hard. We need to go along with the ransom drop that is scheduled for tonight. I am so sorry, Steven. So very sorry you must do this now, but if you want to catch who is responsible for Lulu's murder then this is what we need to do. I will be at your house at 11:00 this evening."

I had no words. I had no thoughts. I was numb. He hung up the phone and an officer led Emily and me to a window that had a drape on the other side. The hall was medicinal and cold. It smelled of mold and the air felt wet. Em was catatonic. She didn't speak a solitary word and her body was trembling. I didn't want to bring her. She shouldn't be here. She grabbed my hand, and she squeezed it. She didn't let go. I could hear her breathing and I could tell she was on the verge of breaking down again. The detective indicated that they were going to pull back the curtain and we would be able to see her body. We needed to verify if it was her or not. In that moment Em let out a small cry. It was as if she knew; she was just waiting, and the waiting was pure torture. I wanted them to just rip the band aid off. We both silently hoped it wouldn't be our Lulu.

The drape was drawn back and instantly we recognized her as our sweet, sweet Lulu. Em let go of my hands and covered her mouth letting out a whimper at first. She then belted an unearthly scream while pounding on the window with her fists.

"No, no, no, no! I want my baby; I want to hold my baby. Please let me be with her. Let me hold her, let me help her. Oh Lulu. Mommy is so sorry Lulu. I'm so sorry."

I tried to grab her and to get her to stop pounding her fists on the glass. The glass shattered and her hands started to bleed, and she was completely unaware. Blood was running down her arms and I grabbed her with as much force as I could, and I held her tight until we both just stood embracing and sobbing uncontrollably.

Other than her pale blue coloring, Lulu looked preserved. Her ID bracelet is still on her tiny wrist. She was missing a boot. Her hair was slicked down and matted. It looked damp and dirty and no longer downy soft and voluminous. Her hands had been scraped up and some of her nails were missing.

They called an ambulance for Emily. She was going to need to be admitted. Emily was mentally disassociated. I don't think she knew what was going on around her. I didn't want to be without her, but I knew it would be best to let the doctors monitor her and let her get some sleep. Even if they needed to sedate her. I didn't want her involved with the news from Sal. For now, I was going to keep this from Em. Angela and Terry went with Emily, and they promised to keep me updated.

I needed to compartmentalize my emotions and my thoughts right now. I needed to put Lulu's death in a pocket and keep it there until I could grieve. Now I needed to find out who did this to her and why. I headed home to meet Sal.

Chapter 7

Bargaining

The fourth stage of grief.

STEVEN

I saw Sal's car in the drive when I returned to the barren house. There was no laughter, no joy. Just pure silence and death. I poured a glass of scotch for each of us and sat at the table. Sal pulled out his file. He had to talk quickly as we had precisely one hour until I had to make the drop. My nerves were shot.

"Steven, I have reason to believe that Monica set the kidnapping in motion. Did you know she had a boyfriend?"

"I've known about him, yes. She indicated it wasn't serious."

"His name is David." Salvatore pulled out an eight by ten photo. I didn't recognize him.

"Sal, I've never seen him before, he never came to the firm. Like I said Monica indicated it wasn't serious. They were both in an open relationship and seeing other people." I was reeling from the events of the evening. I consumed my scotch and poured myself another.

"He is best known for embezzling hundreds of thousands of dollars. People have been looking for him for years. He has been under the radar. He owes a lot of influential people money. Concocting business schemes and taking the investment money and running. He has many aliases. Samuel Cummings, Anthony Genre, and Craig Monroe. I have been following Monica since Lulu's disappearance. The night Lulu went missing, Monica met David at the efficiency suites on Cedar Rd." At this point Sal slid out another eight by ten photo of Monica with David. This time the photo showed the "Monica" I knew all too well. *Jesus Monica you couldn't even bother to shut the curtains. She always wanted someone to watch. This time she got her wish.*

"Did you see Lulu? Was she there?" I was hearing what Sal was saying, but if they were responsible for her disappearance, then where was she when they met up?

"I did not see Lulu."

"Then how can you be so sure that she had anything do to with this?"

"Listen, David's car had a dent on the right-hand side of the car. Very noticeable. I went to the lake this afternoon where they found Lulu. There were skid marks, and you can tell a vehicle had run into the snowbank that was near the lake. It was frozen and could've caused that amount of damage to a vehicle. Also, didn't you say your key witness received a call from an anonymous caller threatening him if he testified? You also indicated that only you and Monica knew that this man was going to testify. In addition, I did some digging and Monica purchased some illegal passports for both her and David. You know my connections, the people I know underground. Isn't this why you hired me? I've also been working with the detectives on the case, we have reason to believe that Monica has no idea about Lulu's death.

Connect the dots, Steven. If I am right, my guess is Monica will be picking up the ransom. David would not convict himself."

What the fuck? "Let's get this money together and head down to the pier. I want answers. You're coming with me." Sal and I took the last gulp of our scotch and headed out the door with the duffel bag in hand. One million dollars. It seemed inconceivable. So much money. My daughter was worth more than a million dollars. A life was taken for the love of money, for someone's selfishness and despair. Lulu paid with her life for my sin. I needed to make Monica and David pay. I was going to do whatever it took to make sure they both suffered. Suffered the way my Emily is suffering, the way my Lulu suffered as she tried to claw her way at the ice to escape the cold and death of the lake. They weren't going to get away with this.

****

I let Sal drive. I was exhausted. I honestly don't know how I was able to get through this. I was doing my best to keep my grief hidden, but it was so hard. I didn't want to let go. My whole body was tense from holding back the tears and my emotions. I knew once I was with Emily I would crumble. I kept seeing my baby girl on that sterile table, motionless, cold, and blue. That image will haunt me for the rest of my life.

The pier was about twenty minutes away. I held on to the duffel bag so tight that my knuckles were white. Sal glanced over at me a couple of times and I knew he was worried.

Submerged

"Can you handle this, Steven? Once we catch her and get her in custody, I will take you to Emily. The authorities will handle it from there."

That's all I wanted, to be with Emily. To hold her and tell her how sorry I was.

"I want that Bitch to rot in hell. I am going to take everything she has, and I am going to ruin her." I could feel heat rising in my chest. I was going to have to contain myself.

"She better pray to God I don't get put in a room alone with her. There is no telling what I might do Sal." I also came to realize that I was going to have to explain to Emily that Monica was responsible, and I was going to have to be up front and honest about our affair. She will never forgive me for this. Never.

"Alright, we're here. Are you ready?"

"Yes." I was ready. I wanted to get this over with. I slowly got out of the car and walked down to the dock where the abandoned Salty Dog sat. I lifted the top of the bench on the stern and dropped the bag inside. As I closed the bench, I checked my surroundings. There was no one in sight. I could hear the crackling ice from the Harbor. It had been just a bit warmer than usual the last two days which caused some of the ice to melt. Some of the boats that sat here in the harbor were unclaimed and rotted. It was dark. Only a single light lit up the dock. I walked back to the car, still being aware of my surroundings. *Where was she? Is she lurking in the dark waiting for me to drive off? Come out you bitch.* I wanted her to come out. I had to see her for myself.

Sal turned the lights off and we waited. Nothing. Around 12:45 we saw a set of headlights on the other side of the bay. It was only for a moment and then the car was gone.

"That's odd. There isn't anything over there, but an old road used for maintenance." Salvatore suspected that something wasn't right. He got out of the car and walked back down to the boat. He lifted the bench cover then slammed it shut.

"Fuck! The bag is gone!" Sal ran back to the car and started the engine. Before I knew it, we were racing down towards the road where we saw the headlights.

"Sal, what's going on? What do you mean the bag is gone?'

"The Money. It's gone. It looks like there was a hole in the bottom of the bench covered by a panel." Sal was focused on the drive.

"That would mean that someone would need to be in the water under the boat to get the bag?" This was inconceivable to me. *The water was freezing. How would someone be under for that long and not suffer from hypothermia?*

We neared the road which was completely covered with snow except for the recent tire tracks from whomever was sitting there, waiting. I could see a body. Someone was lying on the side of the road. It was Monica.

126

Submerged

Salvatore pulled the car over and immediately grabbed his cell phone and gun and exited the car. Instead of checking on the body, he was checking our surroundings. He called the detective, the phone held to his ear by his shoulder and his gun held in both hands, and he gave the police our location. He then called an ambulance. As Sal was talking, I got out of the car and went over to her. She had on a dry scuba diving suit. That would explain her body surviving the cold temperatures. I knelt, felt her neck for a pulse. She had one but it was shallow. I rolled her over and could see that she had been badly beaten. She was almost unrecognizable, but she wore the gold diamond necklace I gave her just weeks before when I told her I planned to divorce Emily. It looked as if she was hit on the head by something. There was nothing else near her. The money was gone. I leaned in as close as I could get to her ear, and I whispered. "I hope you fucking die bitch. And if you don't, I'll make sure it happens."

I stood up and backed away. I could feel myself trembling with anger and sadness. I loved this woman. I was going to give up my life with Emily to be with her. Looking at her battered body I broke down. My day was consumed with loss and now I had to figure out how to put all the pieces back together. I didn't care if she lived or died. I went back and sat in the car until the ambulance arrived.

Sal drove me to the hospital where I could be with Em. He told me he would call me the next day and let me know what was going on. He wasn't giving up on his search for David. He was convinced that

Monica was the key, and he was going to wait until she was awake and question her immediately.

By now I'm sure David was long gone. He had a million dollars. That kind of money can get him far. I'm sure he had every intention of leaving Monica there to die, just as my Lulu died. With her gone there would be no one that would ever know what happened to Lulu or who was responsible even though we had good reason to believe it was David. I wonder if Monica even knew my baby was dead. She must have.

I arrived at the hospital and went to Emily's room. She lay there, sleeping. Content, for now. Angela got up from her seat and embraced me. She cried, I cried. I let it out. All of it. I couldn't hold in my tears any longer. Terry left the room and returned with a nurse and a folding cot, a pillow, and a blanket. I told them to go back to the house and try to get rest. I got it from here. I would never leave Emily, ever again. We had healing to do, and we needed to do it together.

EMILY

I wanted to die. I wanted to be with Lulu. Seeing her in the morgue was an outer body experience. I could see myself screaming, pounding on the glass until it shattered. I had no control over my emotions. My entire world was gone. My husband was with another, and I lost the one thing that kept me going every day. There was no reason for me to go on anymore. The room was dry, and my skin felt itchy from the hospital blanket. No matter how many times the nurse tried to cover me with warm blankets, it didn't help. I found no comfort here. The vexing sounds from the monitors and IV bag rudely interrupted my thoughts and the thick smell of bleach was nauseating. I could see my mom in the hospital room with me. She was talking but I didn't have the energy to listen. Here I was, a drunk. Just like her. Now I was paying the biggest price, the loss of my child and my husband. *Was I going to go crazy like she did? Where was Steven?* I stared at the ceiling, praying, hoping, I would slip away and never wake up.

I was in and out of consciousness. I was emotionally and physically drained and my body couldn't take it anymore. My head was pounding, and I felt sick and depleted. My arms ached from the gashes. This couldn't be happening. My life was beautiful and for a moment, perfect. I dreamt of better days. I drifted off to the memory of the day we were flying high in the sky in the hot air balloon. Now I wish the balloon wasn't tethered and it whisked us far away together. Away from any place we have ever known. Back then the only place I wanted to be was with Steven. Even now, I ached for him. I longed for his strong arms to embrace me and make me feel as though everything else just dissipated. I knew he would take care of me and there was never a time when I thought I would be with anyone else. He was my partner, the one I chose to go through life with. *When did that change for him?* I know I wasn't always easy. I know, now, that I have a problem with drinking, but even now laying here I'm not ready to stop. In fact, I wish they would attach a bag of Jack Daniels to my IV so I could just whisk my mental anguish away. *What did I have to live for anymore?*

****

At some point I had drifted off to sleep and I was awakened by my nurse talking to another nurse as she was changing my IV bag and giving me more antibiotics. She stated that the woman who had been involved with the Van Aken murder was down the hall. I left my eyes shut to give her the illusion that I was still sleeping, but I heard everything.

What the hell? They knew who was involved with the disappearance and murder of my Lulu and it is a woman? What have I been missing?

Once I was sure the nurses had left my room, I opened my eyes.

Submerged

My mom and Terry were gone, and there on the cot next to me was Steven. Asleep.

I silently stared at him. *Where had he been this whole time? Was he in her arms being comforted while I laid here and our Lulu 's lifeless body lay in a refrigeration system at the morgue?* I wanted to reach out to him, wake him up and have him hold me, but I couldn't stop thinking about what the nurse said.

Could the woman the nurses were referring to be Monica? *Who else could it be? She was the one to take her to the theatre.* I sat in the bed and pondered every scenario. I couldn't lay here any longer. I needed to stretch my legs. The anxiety of knowing that the person responsible for the deepest sadness of my life was nearby completely rattled my soul. I quietly slid myself off the bed and stood up. I was a bit unsteady, and I had to take a minute before I could take the first step. I walked down the hall. I needed to know if it was Monica and I wanted answers.

It was late and the hospital was short-staffed. No one even realized I was walking through the halls even though I had my IV pole with me. I walked down the hall and looked in every room until I stumbled upon what I thought was her door. I stood in the doorway. It was dark and I could hear her monitors beeping. I hesitated, and second guessed my instinct to go into the room. *What if this wasn't her?* I was trembling and my breathing felt labored. I relaxed my body, and took a deep breath in. I then started to slowly walk towards the intubated women lying in the sterile hospital bed. I needed to know. *Was this Monica?*

I crept closer and closer to the bed. As I inched closer, I stopped, and paused. My thoughts took me to that day when I came home from my book tour and found her in my kitchen with my husband drinking wine. That was six years ago. Six years she had been plotting and seducing my husband. Six fucking years! I looked at the ungiving person that lay before me and recognized her as Monica.

I leaned in. I leaned in as close as I could. I smelled her and touched her like an obsessed stalker. Her skin was clammy, and she smelled of antiseptics. She was badly beaten, and the machines seemed to be breathing for her. I wanted to whisper in her ear how much I hated her, and I had hoped she felt every ounce of her beating and that she suffered, but I didn't have the energy. For a moment I considered pulling the breathing tube out of her and letting her suffocate as my Lulu suffocated in those freezing waters. I imagined standing here and watching her slip away. Breathlessly. I couldn't bring myself to do it. I was stigmatized by my own judgements and behaviors. In this moment I felt a gentle caress on my shoulder and turned to see Steven. He leaned into me and said, "I got this. Go back to the room."

For the first time in a long time, I trusted him. I trusted his word.

Submerged

I looked him in his eyes without saying a word, turned and walked out of the room. I knew in that moment he would take care of her, and I would never need to think of her ever again.

MONICA

I sat in the water under the pier, not yet submerged by the freezing waters. It was dark and I wanted to see Steven one last time as he dropped the money into the bench. He looked tired. *It's almost over Steven, you'll get Lulu back soon.* My heart was beating so hard that I thought it would come out of my chest. I was nervous yet excited. My adrenaline was pumping throughout my whole body. I was almost there. Almost holding a million dollars. Within a couple of hours, I will be sipping champagne in first class as David, and I fly to Paris. I couldn't believe it was finally happening to me. I was finally going to get the life I deserved. I couldn't wait to see David. It had been five days and that was five days too long.

I watched as Steven walked back to the car. I then swam over to the boat which was only a few feet away. I went under the stern of the boat and gently removed the panel. The duffel bag was heavy. I headed back to the pier and took the waterproof duffel I had hidden. I inserted the money into the waterproof bag, strapped the bag across my body and then put on my mask and went under. I had to swim to the other side of the harbor. David should have dropped off Lulu at the park and by now he would be waiting for me off an old maintenance road.

Submerged

It took me a while to get there. I wasn't a fast swimmer. Once I got to shore, I could hear David calling me in a hushed tone. "Monica, I'm over here."

It was dark, but I followed the direction of his voice. The snow was thick, and I was soaking wet and freezing. There he stood, waiting. He had a blanket and was walking towards me. He flung the blanket around my shoulders.

"Well, where is the bag?" I could tell he was very anxious.

I leaned into him and wrapped my arms around his neck. I went to kiss him, and he pushed me away. "David, what's the matter? It's done. I have the money here in the bag." I pointed to the heavy bag strapped around my body. "Did you drop Lulu off at the park?"

David looked at me and shook his head no.

"What do you mean, no? David what is going on what happened?"

"Shut the fuck up Monica. She is dead Monica. Dead. She has been since the day I took her from the theatre."

"What? No. No you're kidding with me, right? This isn't happening, that wasn't the plan. What did you do David? How did she die?"

"Oh, come on, like you haven't heard. Steven didn't tell you. Tell me, are the cops waiting for me? Did you tell them it was me?"

"I haven't talked to Steven since that day at the theatre. He has ignored all my attempts to speak with him. No, the cops aren't waiting for you. I had no idea, David; I swear no idea."

"I don't believe you. You stupid bitch! Give me the bag!"

David grabbed me and pulled the blanket from around my shoulders. He forcefully grabbed the bag from around my body and yanked it off as well. I fell back onto the ground.

I stood up and faced David and he forcefully grabbed my arms. "David please, you're hurting me, what are you doing? We can still run away together. Let's go. We have everything we need. I don't care about that kid; I don't care about Steven."

David didn't respond. His eyes were dark. In a fit of rage, he came at me and started pounding on my face with his fists.

"You are a worthless whore. I only needed you to do one thing for me. Six years I have tolerated you." His poundings were harder. I couldn't even defend myself as I was exhausted from the swim, and I had lost all energy. Again, someone betrayed me . I loved David wholeheartedly and gave everything to him. I could feel the blood dripping down and I swear I felt my teeth crack. After the first couple of blows I was numb and couldn't feel anything. I started choking on my own blood and couldn't speak. I was numb now and could feel no pain. I wanted to scream I wanted him to stop. In that moment I felt a blunt object hit me on the side of the head and everything went black.

Chapter 8

Anger

The fifth stage of grief.

Submerged

STEVEN

I laid on the cot waiting for Emily to wake up. I couldn't sleep until I talked to her. I wanted to be the first to tell her that Monica plotted to take Lulu. Unfortunately, I overheard the nurses talking and had prayed that Emily didn't hear. It wasn't as if they mentioned her by name, but Emily would know who they were referring to.

I brought Monica into our lives. She took our daughter and schemed to embezzle money from us. Everything that happened was due to my indiscretion and lies. I promised myself that I would make it right with Em. She was my everything. I lost sight of that when giving into my own pleasures and desires.

As I laid there, I could hear Emily get up. When I opened my eyes, she had her back to me. I wanted to speak to her, I wanted to tell her I loved her, but instead I watched. She stood there for a moment, and I could see how unsteady she was. As I started to rise, she started walking. I wanted to see where she was going. I knew she was on a mission to see who the nurses were talking about. I kept my distance from her as she walked solemnly through the halls. She utilized the IV pole as a crutch. It was hard watching her struggle to walk and knowing how she must have been feeling. Seeing her broken and vulnerable made me tremble and I had to hold back my tears. I knew what needed to be done. I knew I needed to show Em how much I was sorry and how much I loved her. Once she got to the end of the hall

138

Emily turned and walked into the room. Her arms bandaged, blood soaking through. I went to the doorway and stood there as Emily faced Monica lying in her hospital bed. I watched as Emily went up to her and leaned in. It looked as if she was whispering something, but I wasn't sure. As she stood straight up, I could see her looking at the tube that was protruding out of Monica's mouth and all the equipment that surrounded her. In that moment I approached Emily and gently touched her shoulder as I didn't want to startle her. She was in a trance. I whispered to her, "I got this."

Em turned, giving me a look I had never seen before. Emily was in there, but these weren't her eyes looking back at me. All I could see was heartbreak and sadness. She slowly walked out of the room.

I went to Monica. I picked up her hand and held it in mine. She was swollen. Her face was almost unrecognizable. I started to squeeze her hand. Tighter and tighter I squeezed. I was incredibly angry, and I wanted to see if she had any sensation, if she could feel pain, because I was feeling pain throughout my entire body. The pain of the loss of my child. The child she took from us. No movement from her. Not even a flinch. I looked at her nails, beautifully manicured, and compared them to those of Lulu's when we saw her in the morgue. The coroner stated in his report that the loss of her nails was due to Lulu clawing her way out of the ice to save herself. My child, my five-year-old beautiful little girl was clawing her way out of the ice just for the ability to breathe. The more I thought of this the angrier I became; at Monica, at myself and at David. How ironic that at this moment I knew what I had to do. I had the ability to make Monica suffer as Lulu did. No one was nearby. The halls were quiet and empty. All I needed to do was twist the hose from the ventilator that was helping her to breathe. Eventually she would suffocate. I picked up the hose and slowly started to twist it. I stared at her, laying there lifeless wishing she would open her eyes so that the last thing she saw was me killing her. I kept twisting it until I was sure it would obstruct all oxygen to her. I then turned and headed back to Emily's room.

Minutes later I heard the alarms and staff running through the halls.

Monica was gone.

EMILY

Once I got back to the room, I crawled into the hospital bed and waited for Steven. It wasn't long before I felt him crawling into the bed next to me and wrapping his arms around me. I didn't resist, I welcomed his touch. He held me tight, and he started to sob. We both cried together. Within minutes I heard a rush of hospital nurses running down the hall and alarms going off.

We both drifted off to sleep and were awakened by the light seeping in from the hospital window. Steven went to get out of bed, but I grabbed him and begged him to stay. At least until the doctors came in. About an hour later the doctor came in on rounds. He checked my wounds and changed my bandages. I could see Steven talking with the physician in the hallway before he left. Steven turned back to me and stated, "we are just waiting for the discharge papers."

"I am hiring a nurse to come to the house to look after your wounds until they fully heal." He looked exhausted. At least I had pain meds that knocked me out and allowed me to sleep. He hadn't slept in days. After what he did, I wasn't sure if he would ever get a good night's sleep again.

"Steven, how are we supposed to plan to bury our child?" I had a lump in my throat, and I started to cry. *Was everyday going to be like this? How was I supposed to go on?*

141

He embraced me. "I'm never leaving your side again. We will get through this together. Your mom and Terry are still at the house and Tonya and Jacob are waiting to see you and help in any way that they can. Mom and Paige will be coming by as well. Let them handle the arrangements."

Steven reached into his pocket and pulled out Lulu's ID bracelet. He opened my hand and placed it in my palm. "She is with us Em."

I didn't know what it was, but holding her bracelet gave me strength. It was as if she was with us, but as I looked back up at Steven all I could feel was anger and distrust. My emotions were all over the place. In one fleeting moment I wanted him to embrace me and never let go and then in another I was repulsed by the sight of him.

The nurse came into the room and disconnected me from the IV. I dressed and Steven put me in a wheelchair to take me home. He had called our driver and Steven sat in the back with me. Never letting go of my hand.

As we approached the house, I came to the realization that Lulu would never be walking through that front door again. I entered the house, and it was quiet. There in the foyer was my mom with her arms stretched out. I went to her immediately and let her hold me. I didn't waiver or flinch from her touch. I don't know what I would do without my mother. I once took care of her, but now she was here, loving me, supporting me, and taking care of me. She was the epitome of what a mother should be, and I was reminded how much I longed for her to be my mom and so grateful that finally we had a bond that was unbreakable. Terry grabbed my bag and took it upstairs.

"What can I do Em?" my mom asked.

"If you could help me run a bath, I would be appreciative." Thank you, mom.

I needed a bath. I still smelled from the hospital, and I just wanted to wash the grief off me.

Just before we ascended the staircase, the doorbell rang, and it startled me.

Steven went to get it, but I was right there, so I answered. It was a delivery.

It had arrived. I had completely forgotten about Lulu's birthday. Today she would have been six years old. We had a big birthday party planned for tomorrow and now we were planning her funeral. I signed for the package and for a moment lost my breath. I started to shake as I ran my hand over the box. It was a very special music box I had ordered from France. It was a unicorn, embellished with gold, and encompassed in a globe of snow. It played Frere Jacques. It was engraved with Lulu's name on a gold plate and there were only five made. It was one of many gifts we were going to give her, but it was the most meaningful to me. I had taught her the song when she just started talking and we sang it every night after story time.

I turned to see everyone looking at me. I didn't want to react.

"Mom, can you help me upstairs?" I didn't want to cry again. I wanted to soak in the hot tub and be alone for a bit.

"Of course." My mom took my arm, and we walked up the staircase together. At the top of the stairs was Lulu's room. Her door was shut. I wasn't ready to go in there just yet. I didn't know if I would ever have the courage to go into her room. I didn't feel worthy of being among her possessions as I felt as though I failed her. I couldn't protect my little girl and now she was gone. I still had the music box in my hand unopened. I placed it on the bathroom counter next to my sink. My mom started to run the water and she helped me remove my bandages from my arms. It was quiet, the steam from the tub clouded us. We didn't need to talk. She knew. She knew me well enough to know that right now I just needed a presence. Someone to be physically there and not speak. She kissed me on my cheek and told me to call her if I needed anything. She slipped out of the bathroom, and I undressed and lowered my body into the bubbled water. I laid back and closed my eyes inhaling the smell of lavender and eucalyptus. When Lulu had a tough time falling asleep, I used the same bubble bath for her. I looked over and stared at the package. *Happy Birthday my sweet Lulu. I Love you so very much and I am so sorry for what you endured. I wasn't there to save you and to protect you.* I slid myself under the water and for a moment considered never coming out. I stayed under as long as I could before I could no longer hold my breath and I came up for air.

I washed my hair and body envisioning the dirt and rotten smell from the last few days being washed away and sucked down the drain. I had hoped it would take my grief along with it. This heavy ache was so much to bear. I soaked until my body looked like a shriveled-up prune and stepped out of the tub drying myself off with a warm towel and wrapping it around my body. I reached for my blow dryer.

I could hear and see Lulu in everything that I did. The warm air blew through my thick wet hair. When I closed my eyes, I could hear her giggling and playing in my room as she often did when I was getting ready for the day. "Look mommy…" My eyes snapped open and emptiness. She was gone. No more loving arms to wrap around my heck. No giggling. No playing.

Then I looked down at his sterile and empty sink. His sink. He did this. They did this. Destroyed what was precious to me.

I let out a curdling scream and thrust the blow dryer at the mirror shattering it into pieces, just as the life I had known was shattered. I was angry. I wanted to just shred something to pieces I wanted someone, something to blame and feel my pain.

I crumbled and fell to the floor and my mom ran to me and held me.

"It's okay, Emily. It will be okay. Let's get you dressed and into bed. I'll bring up some tea."

"I'm so angry. I don't know how to feel anymore. One second, I am so sad and the next I have so much rage. I don't know how to be me anymore. Everything has changed. "

"It's going to take time Emily. You need to grieve. You need to accept what has happened and you need to heal. What you are feeling is normal."

Who was this nurturing woman that sat beside me and caressed my back? My mom came a long way from when I was a little girl. She had so much strength and endurance. I could see her sadness for Lulu, for me, but I could also see and feel her love. It radiated into me, and I remembered what love felt like. I felt so betrayed by Steven and so hurt. I still didn't know the extent of what had happened and why Monica would take Lulu. *Did Monica also kill Lulu and if so, what were the events leading up to her death?*

My emotions towards Steven were mixed right now. I felt love but I felt immense anger as well. I didn't know if I was ready for that conversation. I felt if I were to bring it up that I might lose my shit, again. I was tired and my body ached. For now, I was going to focus on keeping my composure and preparing for the funeral and the wake. I would tuck my anger away and pray it wouldn't resurface. I knew I had a good support team behind me, and I was ready to accept the help they were offering. I needed to take this time to grieve my Lulu. This was for her, and this was for me.

****

We had flower deliveries all day from friends and family sending us their deepest sympathies and condolences. With the doorbell constantly ringing I couldn't relax, and I couldn't stay in bed. I mustered up the energy to get dressed and put on a bit of make-up.

I was doing my best to stay focused on the tasks at hand. I really wanted to drink, but I knew that would cloud my judgment and my feelings. Right now, with the mixed emotions I was carrying I didn't think that drinking would help other than to numb me to what was going on around me. Not to mention, Steven had all the alcohol removed from the house prior to me coming home from the hospital. All except that from my secret stash that I had hidden away in a panel within my walk-in closet.

I headed downstairs to get an espresso. I took it into Steven's office as he indicated he put my laptop there after picking it up from the apartment. I'm not sure why Steven went to my apartment as he never took interest in it before. My laptop would have been fine there, but I am guessing he thought I may have wanted it at home. Writing was my outlet. It brought me joy and was my therapy in times of grief and sadness. I would also wager to say that Steven also wiped my apartment of all alcohol as well.

Submerged

There it was sitting on top of a pile of files that I had assumed were case files from Steven's work; however, upon closer look it was a case file on Monica, and someone named David. I held my espresso and took a long sip. Eyeing the file. Where did Steven get this and how long did, he know Monica was a part of Lulu's disappearance and murder? I picked up the file and went to open it when another paper caught my eye. They were divorce papers. Dated the day before Lulu went missing. Steven was filing for divorce and the paperwork indicated I was an unfit mother due to my excessive drinking and that he was filing for sole custody. A fire ignited in my gut. The rage that I was suppressing was boiling and I was about to explode. *Deep breathes Em, deep breaths.* This was not the time to erupt. This was something I was going to tuck away and save for when it was needed. This was something I had become accustomed to. I would once again bypass this anger and put on a face of sadness and grief. This overwhelming feeling of hatred would rear its ugly head and that was when I would allow it to strike and reveal my revenge. In that moment I knew there was no going back. The thoughts were there. They had overtaken me.

I called Tonya and Steven's sister Paige and asked if they could come by. I wanted to start preparations for everything that needed to get done. I needed something to keep me busy. I wanted to feel useful again. Steven tried to convince me to wait until tomorrow, but I needed to do this. I was repressing the inevitable.

Submerged

My mom and Terry had gone to the cemetery with Steven's mom. Steven's family had a mausoleum and we had discussed whether we would all be buried there as well when our time came. We didn't think Lulu would go first, but she would be laid to rest next to Steven's father. Since we had already known that would be our family's resting spot, I didn't see the need to be present. I did, however, want to be involved in everything else from the casket, the funeral service, and of course the flowers.

I had arranged for my favorite florist to drop off books of arrangements. I told her I would call her with the orders that evening. Tonya arrived and embraced me. We held each other for some time before she let go and wiped away her tears.

"Em you're so strong, and I am so very sorry for your loss. Anything you need, I am here for you. I have been wanting to visit you, but Jacob told me to let you be. He said you would let me know when you needed me, and you did. What can I do to help?"

Tonya was such a great friend, but she had her moments where her love could be overwhelming and sometimes, I had to back away from her. I know her intentions meant well, but she always wanted to be involved, even in matters of my marriage and that was just not her place. This gave her an opportunity to be there for me and I could hold her at arm's length with everything else.

"I had the florist drop off these books of floral arrangements. I need to choose what flowers we will have at the service and for the funeral. I could use your help and expertise in the selection. "I had a general idea of what I wanted, but I knew asking Tonya would give her a sense of purpose as well. She adored my Lulu and always treated her like a princess. Paige was there as well; however, she didn't say much. I always adored Paige. Her sweet mannerism. She didn't make many decisions in her own life, but she loved Lulu as well and I loved Paige as if she were my own sister. Being around her gave me peace and solace. She was like an old soul. Her presence tempered my anger and I felt calm and a sense of serenity.

The three of us sat at the table in the kitchen and I could see Steven and Jacob in the other room talking. Tonya was carrying on and on about flowers and what she thought would be delicate and pretty. I could hear her muffled words as I focused on Steven. I stared at him, as I sipped my iced tea, barely blinking. The sight of him repulsed me and I felt nauseous. Tonya asked, "What were you thinking Em? Did you have any ideas on what type of flower you'd like?"

While staring at Steven I responded to Tonya and said, "Oleanders." My gaze was taken off Steven and I knew what needed to be done.

I could count the number of times Lulu did not sleep throughout the night on one hand when she was a baby. Most of those nights were because she was stuffy or wasn't feeling well. On one occasion she couldn't sleep, and I rocked her in the chair as I watched a movie where an artistically beautiful woman was lied to by her boyfriend, and she murdered him with poison from a white oleander. Granted Ingrid, the character in the movie which I later found out was an adaptation of a book, was crazy and got caught, but she was clever. They movie never indulged on how she used the flower or what the effects were, but I'm sure I could be creative. I wonder, how many people know that flower is deadly? Obviously, no one sitting at this table.

"Oleanders? I have never heard of that flower." She immediately googled them on her phone. She missed the part where it indicates how deadly they were, and she was thrilled to see they came in pink.

"They're not a common flower. I suppose they will have to order them special. Of course, money is no object, whatever I need to do to get them in. I would like white lilies and a sprinkling of pink oleanders on top of her casket." In that moment I felt happy. I had a secret. It was my secret, and no one needed to know. I took another sip of my tea and glanced at Steven. He was looking at me, and mouthed, "I love you." I smiled but more for what I was planning than his words. As far as I was concerned his words meant nothing, but I will play the game. For now. I had to be mindful of Terry. He was a horticulturist, and he may question my choice in flower; however, I will cross that bridge when it is time.

Submerged

Chapter 9

Depression

The sixth stage of grief.

EMILY

Once everyone went home, I called the florist to get things ordered. It was a little late, but she had been a good friend of mine that I met years ago in yoga class, and she told me to call no matter the time. She gave me some push back on the oleanders even stating that they're beautiful but very poisonous and she wasn't sure if she would be able to get them in time. Of course, friends or not, money speaks volumes, and I offered her whatever she needed to get them in.

I hung up with her and grabbed my blanket and sat on the porch swing. My favorite place to be. I loved the cold brisk air, and it reminded me of my Lulu. Unlike many other children, winter was one of Lulu's favorite times of the year. She loved the snow and playing in it. She loved snuggling up by the fire afterwards in her pajamas with homemade hot chocolate. Her cheeks would be rosy, and she would stare longingly into the flames. Mesmerized.

Steven came out.

"May I join you?"

"Sure." Although deep inside I wanted to be left alone. I decided to take this opportunity to see what exactly had happened to Lulu and see what other secrets he may have been hiding. My disposition and thought process completely changed when he came out.

Submerged

"I think I'm ready to hear what happened. Please tell me how Lulu died. How was Monica involved?"

"Em, I'm not sure we should talk about this now. Perhaps after the funeral."

His voice was a bit condescending, and it bothered me. Even now he was trying to control how I felt and what I needed.

"NO STEVEN! I want you to tell me now. No more tiptoeing around me. Stop trying to protect my feelings. If you were so concerned about them then we wouldn't be in this situation. I know about your affair. I've known it for years. I also know you filed for divorce the day before Lulu went missing. According to you, I am an unfit mother and you wanted sole custody of our daughter. Imagine how I felt to discover those papers as I was preparing to plan our daughter's funeral. All the secrets you keep from me. All the lies."

He didn't utter a word. It was as if I sucked the life right out of him.

Adulterated evil starts out as a lie. The equivalent to a small wound. Small enough where you think it is innocent and *what difference will it make,* until that wound irritates and starts to fester with each scratch and touch. Once you attempt to forgive that lie, a scab will form but it never fully heals as it is picked at and becomes mangled until once again you are left with an unhealed never-ending pustulous sore of deceit which never heals but grows until the surrounding skin becomes gangrenous and necrotic and needs to be removed leaving a scar. A scar that is a constant reminder of the pain that was endured. I didn't want a scar. I wanted to erase the pain as if it never occurred.

"What about you Emily? Always skirting away to your apartment to get drunk. The many nights I came home to find you passed out on the couch with an empty bottle. What if Lulu woke up throughout the night and needed you? You were in no condition to take care of our child. You are a drunk and I had to protect her."

His words hurt but it was something I already knew. I had been beating myself up for years over my alcoholism. I knew it became a problem when I couldn't go one day without it. It was a coping mechanism for me. I knew my marriage was falling apart right before my eyes and there was nothing, I could do to save it.

"Do you think for one second that I didn't know I had a problem? I hate myself for who I have become. This is just a shell of me. Your neglect and your late hours left me lonely. I was lonely Steven. I needed you and rather than helping me or asking me what I needed you would leave. I only had you and Lulu. You both were my forever, and I couldn't stand losing what we had. Now Lulu is gone, and I lost you too."

I was crying. I was crying because this conversation wasn't going as I had planned. I am pronouncing my undying love for a man who fell out of love with me years ago and now all I wanted to do was seek revenge and kill him. I feel like I lost myself and I'm now losing my mind. I could not control this hurricane of emotions.

He leaned in and wrapped his arms around me. He kissed me softly on the cheek and said, "Emily, I am so sorry. I will tell you everything you want to know."

He proceeded to tell me about his relationship with Monica from when they were in high school and the miscarriage to when he came home for his father's funeral. He even went into detail about their escapades and having Monica into our home when I was away at the apartment. He left nothing out. He then proceeded to tell me how he hired Salvatore the day Lulu went missing and how Salvatore uncovered the truth about Monica and that she was only with Steven to break up our marriage and kidnap Lulu for ransom.

"It is Salvatore's understanding that Monica was not aware of Lulu's death based on Monica's actions during the time we were to drop off the ransom. Salvatore was watching her closely to see if she had any contact with David, which she did not. That's when we made the drop and discovered Monica's body on the other side of the harbor. As you know she was beaten, and we believe it was David who did it. I killed Monica in the hospital Em. I did that for you. She was a dirty bitch who planned to hurt us, and she was the ultimate reason we lost Lulu."

No Steven, you were the ultimate reason we lost Lulu. You allowed her into our lives. You fucked her in my home, and you

allowed her to spend precious time with our daughter. Time you
should have been spending with her.

I had to compose myself once again. I had to make Steven
believe I was eating this all up. I had to make him feel like the man. I
hated myself for being this fake person. I had to be weak, I had to
make him feel like he was in control of this conversation.

"I know you killed her for me. For us. She deserved what she
got and may she rot in hell. You didn't deserve to be lied to and
mistreated as you were."

I felt as if I was possessed as I said these things to Steven for, I
wanted him to rot in hell with her. In the same moment, my anger
turned to lust. I wanted him inside me. My emotions were all over and
I felt like I was in a tornado of love and hate. My body was
overflowing with an urge to grab him, sit on him, and take him in. I
put my hand on his dick, and he looked at me. He took my hand and
pressed down on it and leaned in to kiss me. I got off the porch swing
and kneeled on the ground in between his legs and slowly started to
unzip his pants. The wind blew and it was cold, but his dick was rock
hard. I slowly eased it into my mouth looking at him and never taking
my gaze away as I took him deeper and deeper in my mouth. *I wonder*
if this is how Monica did it. Did she look at him, did she even give
blow jobs? He moaned and pushed my head into it. I gagged, and
slowly released him from my mouth. I then stood up and straddled
him. I wanted to be fucked. Hard.

Submerged

I whispered into his ear, "Take me inside- Fuck me."

He picked me up and took me inside- he thrusted me on the couch and got completely naked. I undressed for him and spread my legs slowly touching myself, inviting him in and he did as I requested. I clawed at his back, and he pressed his lips deep into my mouth. He then kissed me down my navel and into the wettest part of my body where he licked me until I dripped my sweet cum into his beautiful face. I then begged him to bend me over and fuck me doggy style. I didn't want it to end. I felt in some small way like I needed to be punished. Punished for my thoughts of murder and hatred. There was a mirror in the living room and as he bent me over, we both looked into it watching ourselves fuck like wild animals. We ended up on the floor, where he slowed down and started to make love to me. I couldn't resist it. Even though I hated him so much I still wanted some type of love from him.

"I want to cum inside of you. Let's have another baby Em. Let's start over." He released himself and I didn't push him away. It was warm and I could feel it running throughout my body.

We both relaxed and didn't move, we were silent. Listening to each other breathe. I didn't want to talk anymore. This was all too much, and I was very confused. Eventually we fell asleep where we were, and I woke before Steven. I lay there staring at him. He looked so innocent, so peaceful. He was quiet and still. In this moment it reminded me of our early days in college when I knew I was his only love. I would often catch him staring at me with a smile on his face and I was aware of his love for me. In this moment I was taken back to all the love I had for him. I was in a trance of nostalgia, thinking of every good memory we shared in our life. These thoughts were only memories, shadowed by what has transpired. Now that I knew everything I didn't waiver from my plan. I thought, making love, and sharing this moment and time with him would make me change my mind, but it didn't.

****

Grief overcame me in waves. I was in a tunnel of daydreams and emptiness. I couldn't decipher one day from the next and it felt like there was a hole where my heart once felt warmth, love, and joy. How do you wrap your head around burying your child?

It was the day of the funeral. Everything was taken care of, and the oleanders were spectacular. When Terry saw them, he commented on what an odd choice for a flower. He gave me a look of concern but didn't say much more about it.

Steven hadn't left my side since we made love. He was doting on me every second. His felicitations made my stomach churn. He was unaware that he was failing at his constant need to make me happy, to make me forget what he did to me. Internally I was clawing at my insides dying to release my anger. For now, I smiled, and made him believe his charm held the same effect it had on me that first night I met him at the college party.

Submerged

God, I wanted a drink. I missed it. The way the smooth whiskey just glided down my throat and made me feel warm. The first glass is the best glass. It's the one that makes you feel good. Numb, relaxed. The second, you start to feel invincible, giddy. As if all your dreams and ideas will come to fruition. The third, you start to feel regret, but you say to yourself, "fuck it, it's my life and I deserved this." Anything after three, well if you can remember how you feel after three, then good for you. That's where I wanted to be. Blacked out. Numb. Being here, at this moment, didn't seem real. It was an outer body experience and I felt as though I had no control over my emotions. I saw myself at the casket, leaning over Lulu, sobbing. I couldn't bring myself to leave her, and when the casket was closed, I could see myself falling into a million pieces. *This couldn't be happening. I'm not supposed to bury my little girl.* It was all just a vague memory. As if I was alone with her in the room. Just Lulu in her casket and me standing there. I couldn't see or hear anything else around me, only the buzzing white noise in my ears. I didn't want comfort. I didn't want anyone to touch me. I just wanted to be with her. As I mourned, my body welled with revenge. I wanted nothing more than to make those who were responsible pay for this. My thoughts took me to deep valleys of anger and hatred. The embers were hot, and it was only a matter of time before they erupted.

Before Lulu's casket was put into the mausoleum, I made sure to remove the flowers. I insisted that I wanted to keep them, and no one thought that was unusual. After all, I was her mother. I held onto those oleanders with everything I had. Never letting them go. They were my weapon of revenge. They were the only thing keeping me calm at that moment.

*****

I had no desire to speak to anyone once we returned home. I immediately headed to my room. I wanted to wallow in my sadness and grief, and I didn't want to move. Every thought, every memory of Lulu came flooding over me. I couldn't stop the tears. I could feel my body trembling and once again it felt as if I wasn't me. I felt as though I had transcended into an abyss of delirium. I was in and out of consciousness. In an instant I seemed to snap out of the black hole I was in, and I was laying in the bed. Steven was lying with me staring at me with a look of shock and disbelief on his face, his hands tightly gripped around my wrists. It hurt. I had no recollect of lying down or of Steven coming into my room. *Was I talking with him? What did I say?*

"Steven, what's happening? I'm sorry, I'm not myself." I grabbed him and pulled him in. He started crying and I just held him.

Submerged

STEVEN

I told her everything. I didn't hold back, and I was forthright in all my intentions. Monica pleasured me and she addressed me like the man in control. She needed me and I was there for her, but I know now that it wasn't real. Over six years I spent with a woman whom I had longed for and with whom I loved, and I was willing to leave my wife for, but she deceived me. She created a plan to kidnap my child to get a ransom, and now my child was dead, and it was all because of her.

There were moments when I grieved her. And there were moments that I hated what I did to Monica. I loved her for so long and she hurt me. She destroyed me. That is how I justified killing her. I had nightmares of her coming to me, laying with me, and seducing me, then begging for me to not kill her as I wrapped my hands around her neck and watched the life just drain from her soulless body. I would awake in cold sweats. She was evil. She haunted me.

I wanted to start over. When I saw Em on the back patio, I took that moment to be honest with her. I was reminded of what I needed in my life. God, she felt good. I wanted to love her and fuck her like I used to before Monica. I wanted to plant my seed within Em once again so we can have another baby. *How or why did I fuck this up with her?* What was I hoping to gain? Emily was established, she was funny, she was amazing, yet here I was looking for something more. I

163

was and I am an idiot. I internally planned to fix it. To try to make amends, no matter what it took.

I was in constant touch with Salvatore. He was good at his job, and I knew if anyone could track down David it would be him. Salvatore had a lead, and we had a good idea as to where David was hiding. It was just a matter of time until we found him. At that point I would spare no expense. I had every intention of hiring a hit man and Salvatore already put me in contact with her. Knowing how David worked, a woman would be the only thing enticing enough for him to trust. I kept this from Emily. I didn't want her to know. It was one less thing for her to think about and I wanted to protect her at all costs.

Emily wasn't the same. I would find her daydreaming and just staring at nothing. Most of the time it was as if she was a zombie, going through the motions and smiling as if she was "on queue." I had made sure my staff had wiped the house and her apartment of all alcohol. I'm sure she was missing her nightly glass of whiskey, but it was what was best for her. I needed to help her to be sober even though she didn't talk to me about it. It was what was best for her, and I was going to make sure I didn't screw things up again. She may hate me now for taking away her escape but one day she would thank me. I already put an end to Monica. I killed her for Emily. Now I was going to rescue Emily from herself and make sure that David suffered as well.

Submerged

Laying our sweet Lulu to rest was unimaginable. I could not conceive of putting her in a concrete box next to my father. Emily was beside herself. She would not allow any of us to console her and she held tight to the flowers that laid upon Lulu's casket. I was concerned about Em.

I don't know where I would have been in this moment without my mom and Paige. They both stood by me through all of this. I needed someone I could go to during this time. I considered staying with them and giving Em her space. I knew Angie and Terry were in town, so she wouldn't be alone, but I needed to be with her. I was just struggling with my own demons. I couldn't cope with what I had done. With what I was planning to do to David.

I was alone. Alone in my thoughts and alone in general, but I couldn't leave Emily again. That is how this entire mess happened. I left her. Lonely.

When we came home from the funeral Emily went immediately to her room. I politely excused myself from Angela and Terry and went to be with her. As I entered her room she was lying in her bed, in the fetal position. She was sobbing uncontrollably. I didn't know what to do. I wanted to go to her and comfort her, but I hesitated, and I waited. I watched as she sobbed, and I felt an immense need to be near her. To hold her and to comfort her. I laid down next to her. Gently. I slowly spooned her and wrapped my arms around her shaking body. It was quiet. Only the sounds of her sobs echoed within

165

the room. She then stopped and she said, "I don't know you. I don't trust you. I don't know if I can go on being your wife." I didn't speak. I didn't know how to respond. This upset her. I had never seen Emily like this before. She abruptly turned and started to push me away. She was pounding on my chest while screaming that she hated me and that she blamed me. I couldn't take it anymore and I retaliated against her.

"Stop it! Emily, I can't do this. I'm sorry. I fucked up, yes, I fucked up. But I killed her. I did that for you. How many times do we have to go over this? What do I need to do to make it right?!" I was so angry that I had unconsciously grabbed her wrists and I was grabbing them so tightly that I could see marks forming.

She stared into my eyes with a blank stare, and said, "You could die. I want you to die."

I couldn't believe what she was saying. *Did she hate me this much?* I stared back at her and couldn't respond. In an instant she snapped out of it. The light was brought back to her eyes, and she put her hand on my face gently caressing it and stated, "I'm so sorry Steven, I didn't mean that. I am so confused; I am so sad. I don't know what I am saying anymore." She then proceeded to wrap her arms around me and pull me to her. There was nothing I could do but hold her back and sob.

Chapter 10

Acceptance

The seventh stage of grief.

EMILY

Days passed, and I didn't have the energy to leave my room. I was reeling between withdrawals and grief. I barely ate. Steven had gone back to work, and mom and Terry returned home. Vivian would check in on me from time to time. I often heard conversations she had with the staff on the other side of the door. She would instruct them to let her know if I had left my room. Before my mom left, she came to my room. She lay next to me in the bed, and she held me. We didn't talk and I knew this was her way of telling me she loved me. She never mentioned my drinking, nor did she ever mention her history of alcoholism. I imagine Lulu's death was just as hard for her as it was for me, and she was probably fighting her own demons to not only stay sober but to focus on her mental well-being.

I had meticulously placed the oleander flowers in a silk satchel which I placed under my pillow. For now, they were my most prized possession and they were the only thing giving me hope and bringing any type of joy to my days. I hadn't quite figured out how to use them. I spent my days and nights calculating and brainstorming a plan. Christmas was nearing and I had to step out of this room and attempt to have some resemblance to life. I didn't even know if I wanted to go on living anymore. Not without Lulu. If I wanted to successfully follow through with my plan, I needed to propel myself into existence again and show Steven that I was capable of being sober and of being myself; whomever that may be.

I glanced over at my vanity where the packaged music box still sat. I still hadn't opened it. I was waiting. I decided I was going to move the music box and the silk sack into my secret cubby space in my closet. The one where I had hidden a brand-new bottle of top-shelf whiskey. For now, I had to be clear minded so that I could perform the ultimate task of cleansing my life and ridding it of this fetid and foul evil being that resided in my home. I needed to shake it off and get into a routine again. I needed to rise from these ashes of grief and do something. My agent and publishing company had been very gracious with the extensions and allowed me time to grieve. I was thankful for the break, but this would be the perfect time for me to throw myself into my work and create a new story. One that could take my readers on a journey they would never forget. I reached for my phone and texted Gary.

I need a distraction and I am ready to get back into the game. When can we meet to discuss a new novel idea?

I needed a shower. I turned the water on to give it time to get hot. Standing at the sink I could barely recognize the woman whose reflection stared back at me. Bags under my eyes and mascara masking my face like a raccoon. I don't remember the last time I washed my face or even brushed my teeth. It's taking everything in me to rise. To breathe. Looking in the mirror and staring at the shell of my empty soul, I'm reminded of days past. Making love in the library corridors, laughing so hard my stomach hurt, the agonizing pain and joy from giving birth, my little girls giggles, and hugs to the sorrow I felt that day. The day my world changed. Now the room is still. No life, no happiness. Just a blanket of gray surrounded by a sea of blackness which has now filled my heart. I could feel myself drifting once again into the black abyss of madness. It was like a switch. One moment I had hopes of a brighter day and the next I just wanted to die.

I was startled by the ring of my cell phone. It was Gary.

"Gary, that was fast. Thank you for calling me back."

"Emily, I didn't expect to hear from you so soon. The agency is behind you. I'm glad you're ready to get back to work but I want to make sure that, you're ready."

Gary was a flamboyant yet successful agent in the literary world. He was just starting out when I met him and together, we became a force to be reckoned with. He was more than an agent; he was a friend. He knew most of my dark secrets and was aware of my drinking. He often tried his own attempts at an intervention, but he knew I wouldn't seek the help until I was ready. He was patient with me and even though I procrastinated on several projects he knew he could depend on me to get him something substantial and worthwhile. In the end, making us a powerful team, making the New York Times Bestselling list six times.

"I have never been more ready. My thoughts are just reeling with ideas, and I need a distraction. Steven has concerns. Let me work on things at home and I will be in touch."

I knew I couldn't seem too eager. *How would this look when Steven fell to his demise?*

"I will e-mail you, my ideas. I am eager to meet in person, and I miss you dear friend."

Gary agreed and with that I felt confident that I had sealed a plan for my next novel.

I took a shower and generously lathered my body with the most sensual body butter. I massaged it in and took my time getting dressed. It felt good to be clean. I felt refreshed, renewed.

For the first time since I locked myself in my room, I opened the blinds and squinted at the bright sunshine glistening from the white snow. It was breathtaking. I opened the window a bit and breathed in that brisk smell of winter, closing my eyes, and slowly inhaling it. I imagined a new beginning.

******

The only way I could get out of this God forsaken prison was to agree with Steven and Vivian that I would attend AA meetings. I had to play along. I had to let them see I was capable of being on my own without resorting to alcohol. If I were going to meet with Gary, I had to make every attempt to prove I could be sober and clear minded.

Luckily for me my driver was someone with whom I had formed a bond with early on. Charlie. He was a sweet young man. He knew of Steven's indiscretions. He knew the torment I went through for six years watching my husband cheat on me.

I only agreed to attend meetings if Charlie drove me.

While Steven and Vivian were adamant about my sobriety, I was still in denial. However, my withdrawals were becoming more noticeable to me, and they were more than I could bear. I hid it all too well. I was good at masking my feelings. I broke down in the solace of my own company when no one was around. I was suffocating with the constant attention from Steven and Vivian. They followed me wherever I went and chaperoned me on trips outside of the home. We would exchange pleasantries, but the conversations were never substantial. No one ever asked how I was doing. It was as if the versions of them I once knew disappeared when my Lulu was gone. Without Lulu there was no Emily. Their lives seemed to go on and thrive. They didn't know how to confront conflict and change. Instead, they stripped the house and my apartment of all remnants of alcohol and brushed it under the rug. I was left to deal with the grief as well as the mental and physical anguish of failure. I know if I could just have one drink, everything would be okay.

I agreed to attend regular AA meetings of their choice. They were clear on the "rules." Rules, I only entertained because I knew what was coming. I pretended to be eager and meek, carefully listening to what they wanted me to do. Happily obliging. Charlie had to take me to and from the meetings and nowhere else. The meetings were held in a rundown church. I could see the many alcoholics anxiously waiting to enter the dilapidated building. Chain-smoking and polluting their lungs with vile poison. Happily exchanging one addiction for another. The irony of it all is the church was located across the street from the same dingy liquor store I visited every week. Outside on the sidewalk, was my favorite cashier Susan, taking a smoke break of her own. She saw me get out of the car and I didn't try to hide. I nonchalantly looked her way and waived. I then yelled, "I'll see you later!" I had no intention of getting sober, I just needed to get out of that damn house and breathe again.

The meetings were held in the basement. It was damp and smelled of moth balls and musty towels. The coffee was percolating, and the donuts looked like remnants of day-old bakery. Stale and dry. How could anyone get sober when the environment was clad with depression and somberness?

I scoped out the room. Metal folding chairs placed in a circle so we could all face one another and confront our demons. Admit our faults and failures. Repent and ask for forgiveness for being the horrible alcoholics that we were. If Lulu was still here, if I had something to live for, I would take this very seriously. Now at this precipice of time in my life I wanted to be the bad guy. I didn't want to get better. Why should I have a life when hers was taken? I'm going down, but not until I get what I want.

Submerged

I watched as people started flowing in. Some disheveled and still high or drunk. Others treating it as your typical weekend gathering with friends. Chatting it up about family and work, as if they weren't struggling to be sober. And then there is that one person. There is one in every gathering, whether it is a family get together, staff meeting, or even an AA meeting. There is always that one person that thrives to be the first one to chirp up and announce their mishaps, and ill feelings. There is always one person that craves attention whether positive or negative. They had this gnawing voice telling them they had to be the first one to proclaim their faults. I spotted her. I knew them all too well. I had a gift for analyzing a room. It came with my ability to pay attention to detail when watching my surroundings. This was how I built character development for my books.

She was overweight, semi slumped in her chair, but her eyes were darting everywhere. She made eye contact with me and smiled- a shy but confident smile. Her eyes kept moving towards the door anticipating the arrival of the chairperson responsible for organizing this meeting. She had red hair. It was a natural red. Messy, and wind-blown her curls pointed in every direction. She cupped a Styrofoam cup of coffee, and I could only imagine that she thought it was something stronger. *What was she thinking? How was she feeling? Was she truly an alcoholic or here for company, attention, and stale donuts?* The chairs filled quickly, and people were chatting with one another. Welcoming each other back and ogling the room to see who was new and who wasn't. Many eyes came my way. I didn't look like

174

any of the other members of the meeting. I imagined it was because I didn't live in the city, and I was from a more influential town in Boston. The suburbs didn't offer much as far as AA meetings were concerned. I smiled and sat with my legs crossed and my hands gently folded on my lap. I was ready. Ready to hear frumpy "Annie" speak and proclaim her life story of tragedy and chaos.

A middle-aged man entered the center of the circle and asked everyone to take a seat and get comfortable.

"Hi everyone. My name is Allen, and I am an alcoholic. I have been sobered for eight years. I see a few fresh faces. Please know that this is a safe space. A space where you can listen, speak, and express what you are going through. I encourage you to share your story. It is through communication that we heal."

Allen was a stout man with bowed legs. He smelled as though he bathed in his cologne and just got out of the shower. His face and smile were warm, but not warm enough for me to share. Frumpy Annie was grinning from ear to ear and staring at Allen. She was smitten. I couldn't help but chuckle while watching her swoon.

In the corner of the room, I saw a woman. She wore sunglasses and her head was covered with a silk scarf. She didn't join the group, but she stood in the dark corner and when I wasn't looking at her, I could sense her stare. It made the hairs on my arms stand straight up and made me uneasy. Perhaps it was another suburban mom who was

175

trying to be conspicuous. The next time I looked over at her she was gone.

Shortly after, the meeting was over, and I was more than happy to escape.

I bee lined for the door and then paid a visit to Susan before getting into the car.

Just a little swig was all that I needed. Something to take the edge off. I purchased a small bottle of tequila and poured it into my lemon lime hydration water. Two birds and one stone. I asked Charlie to take the scenic route home and he was more than happy to oblige.

I had a gentle buzz by the time I returned home. As Charlie pulled into the drive, I saw a car parked down the road with a silhouette of someone sitting in their car. Normally I wouldn't find this suspicious except we lived in a rather small community, and I knew everyone that lived on our street. This was not a car that I recognized. Before I could look any further Steven was meeting me at the door.

"Emily where have you been? Your meeting ended hours ago."

"Jesus Steven. Give me room to breathe. I asked Charlie to take me for a ride. I am doing what you asked. Stop punishing me!"

I was done. Done with this marriage, done with trying to be someone I wasn't. I was missing Lulu. She was my glue. She was my sanity.

Submerged

Before entering the house, I turned one last time and the car was gone.

STEVEN

I was reeling from the funeral as well as taking care of Emily and orchestrating the demise of David. If Emily and I were going to have any resemblance of a life together, she had to get sober. I tried to repress the fact that she indicated she wanted me to die. She loved me. I know this. Those words stung but they were said out of frustration and anger.

I went back to work shortly after the funeral; however, I couldn't concentrate on anything. I thought diving back in would be a nice distraction, but it only led me to dark thoughts about Monica.

One afternoon it had gotten so bad that I had to step out of the office and get some fresh air. I decided to take a walk among the city streets. As I was walking, I noticed this woman in front of me. She was built like Monica and walked like her. From the back I was convinced it was her. In that moment I felt relief. Relief that I didn't kill her. I walked faster to catch up to her, anticipating a reunion where I could get answers. She could tell me why. *Why would you allow our affair to go on for six years, allowing me to feel that our arrangement was okay and that you truly loved me, only to deceive me the way that you did?* I caught up to her and gently tapped the back of her shoulder. The woman turned around and very quickly I realized it was not Monica. The woman was irritated and distraught. I apologized, indicating I thought she was someone else, and I headed back to the office.

Monica continued to haunt me.

I hated her, and I suppressed so much rage towards her, but I missed her too. Every time I went into the office, I could see her standing, waiting for her coffee. Turning and glancing my way as I passed her. Smiling and gently brushing her hair out of her eyes.

I missed our lunches and longed for her touch. I longed to touch her hair and caress her beautiful face. She had this way about her that drew me in. I couldn't resist. I had to have her and now I missed her. I missed how she felt when I was inside of her, and I missed how she told me how much she appreciated me and loved me. She adored me and she wanted me.

Monica didn't re-enter my life until it was too late. I wanted to leave Emily sooner, but if I abandoned Emily, I abandoned Lulu. I couldn't be that father. I did what I could do to have both. Now with the death of Lulu I am left with the guilt of these feelings, but I can't help but still want to be with her. Even after her role in Lulu's death.

Many nights I held Monica in my arms in my bed. I knew she loved me. I felt it. There were moments when we made love, and she would cry. She expressed that I was her person. I was the one that would rescue her from everything evil. She would express how she never stopped loving me and that she wished we had our child together. Maybe, just maybe, it would have changed the outcome of our current situation. She would never deliberately hurt my Lulu. It was David.

It's just me and Em now. *How can we start over? Is there hope or are we going to be in this endless tug of war of blame and unhappiness.* There was nothing tying me to Emily any longer other than the memory of the love we once had. I wanted her to be well and I insisted on continuing to get her help. She has not been very happy with the idea of me having someone with her everywhere she went. I wish she would see it was for her own good. I have seen indications of mental instability within her. As if she is hallucinating or talking to herself. I am worried if someone isn't with her that she may hurt herself. I had learned through my own therapist that I couldn't save Emily. She would need to recognize her addiction and get help on her own. I still felt the need to continue to watch over her and ensure she was taking those final steps towards sobriety. Reluctantly she agreed to go to meetings if our driver Charlie took her. He was a confidant and friend to her, and I wanted her to be comfortable. I wanted her to succeed and get well so we could move forward. I had to accept that her sobriety was in her hands and only hers.

****

Weeks turned into months and Emily, and I were going through the motions. We were roommates at best. Both of us were working on ourselves through therapy and counseling. Emily was continuing to attend meetings and she seemed content. She was reclused. Often going to her room. I had created a home office for her so she could work on writing again. She expressed that she had been in contact with her agent, Gary, and she was planning on starting a new novel. This came as a surprise to me, but I knew this was her outlet. I made the decision to terminate her lease for her apartment. I didn't see the need for her to go away to write when she had ample space in our home. I was at the office most of the time so there were no distractions. She was visibly upset when I gave her the news, but afterwards she indicated it was for the best. She was making progress and I wanted to ensure that we would reconnect on her terms and when she was ready.

****

It was a Saturday, and I was sitting in my office at home. I had a few loose ends to tie down on a case on which I was working.

The ring of my cellphone startled me. It was Sal.

"David, our informant located David. He was in Parikia, Greece. Upon her arrival she found he had fallen to his own demise. A single gunshot wound to the head. Suicide. Next to him lay an envelope addressed to Emily Van Aken. I am assuming it is his suicide letter. A currier will be by this afternoon to deliver it."

I was speechless. His guilt must have gotten the best of him. Why write to Emily? His last words were written to her.

181

Submerged

Just as I hung up the phone Emily came into my office.

"Hi. I was hoping we could spend time together this evening. I just feel like I'm ready to talk and reconnect. I'm so tired of feeling hopeless, scared, and lonely. I just want to be near you. I want to cook for you tonight and enjoy a nice dinner together. Are you available?"

The sunlight was beaming through the windows, and it shined on her. Making her brown eyes glisten. In this moment I saw all of Em's beauty and I was captivated by this amazing woman who stood before me. She looked healthy and she looked like my Em. *Can we really get through this?*

"I would love to have dinner with you. I've missed us Em. I've missed you."

"I have missed us too. I want to start over. I want to be with you throughout our days Steven. I hate that we have been so distant and not there for one another. I love you."

I hadn't heard those words from her in years. She walked out of the room, and I felt for the first time in a long time a sense of new beginnings. I waited for so long for her to see that I was sorry. Sorry that I was an awful husband, and I wasn't there to support her as I should have been. I disappointed her by not living up to the promise I made to her that beautiful sunny day on the hot air balloon. I can still recall the words I whispered in her ear that day. "Emily Brooks I will be yours forever and you will never want for anything. You will never be alone again. I am yours, always."

182

Submerged

I decided to take David's letter to dinner. We would read it together and close this chapter

Submerged

Chapter 11
Revenge

EMILY

I spent weeks and months appeasing Steven. Showing him, I was attempting to become sober, never wavering from my deep thoughts of revenge. I even fooled myself thinking that those thoughts and emotions would dissipate after time, and I would no longer want to end his life. However, he always showed his true colors. When I had indicated I was in contact with Gary to start a new novel he ended my lease at my apartment. He took away my escape. That was the one true place where I could focus and not think about Lulu. It was hard to write when my emotions were suppressed around my baby girl and the guilt I felt. Everywhere I looked within our home I was reminded of her. She had never been to my apartment. In fact, Lulu always referred to my apartment as my office. It was a safe space for me and from my deep dark thoughts. The home office Steven created for me provided no inspiration. Now that spring was here, I could take my laptop to a park and focus on writing. I spent many afternoons with my laptop and a good park picnic table. Afterwards Charlie would take me to see Susan so I could escape once more before going home.

As morbid as it seems, one of the only things that brought me pure solace and calm was visiting Lulu in the Mausoleum. It was the only place I had zero desire to drink. I was always sober when I went to her sacred place. I went as often as I could, and I always took pink roses and daisies. These were picked from our lush gardens. The same garden where Lulu took her first steps. I could vividly hear her giggles as the blades of grass tickled the bottoms of her feet. The sun was beaming that day, but the breeze was simply perfect enough so that we wouldn't feel the uncomfortableness of the heat. She had on the cutest little pink romper with a floppy sun hat. The strap just gently cinched below her jaw. Her curly brown hair darting out from the bottom. I had laid a blanket on the ground, white with delicate yellow flowers, and I sat upon it with Lulu. We snuggled and she crawled a bit. I watched as she slowly stood. She was leaning on me, trying to balance herself and she stepped forward towards a blue bird. "Bird, bird mommy." I sat and let my precious little girl, who was just as delicate as the flowers on the blanket, manifest into this fearless creature, on a search for all things wonderous in the world. It was a glorious day.

Charlie dropped me off at the cemetery, but he was kind enough to give me the solace I needed, and I told him to be back in 30 minutes. Our family plot was inside a magnificent building adorned with stained glass windows, and our own area for prayer. I approached where my Lulu was, and noticed fresh flowers laid at her site. Lillies. White. Vivian and Paige must have stopped by, but they generally brought Lulu white roses. Predictable. Perhaps they were feeling like a change. Regardless, it brought a smile to my face. Lulu was loved. I placed the flowers in the vase and sat on the bench directly in front of where she lay. I gently placed my hand on her site, and closed my eyes as I always did. *My baby girl, I'm here. I miss you more than you know. I dream of you often, and often think of how I was not there that day. The day when you went away. If I ever disappointed you, I am so sorry. I tried, Lulu. I tried to be the mom you wanted and needed me to be. I feel like a failure. You bring me peace and I wish I could bottle up this feeling and grab ahold of it every time I had a negative thought. I haven't been myself Lulu. I feel like I am losing my mind. I know if you were still here, I would be given the strength to be sober for you. I was so selfish, thinking of what I lost with your father. I used it as an excuse to justify my drinking. To justify my pain. I want to die. Even now. What do I have? I want to be with you on the other side.*

I opened my eyes, as they were burning from the tears. I snatched a tissue from my bag and gently wiped them away. In pure ritualistic behavior, I rose, and walked towards the matches and candles so I could light a candle for my Lulu. I noticed the woman I saw at the AA meeting in the dark corner with the silk scarf and sunglasses. She was kneeling in the pew, facing our Lord who hung on the cross. She was praying. I couldn't see her face, but I knew it was her. *Why was she here?* I didn't hear her enter. There was something familiar about her. I just couldn't put my finger on it, but I felt this incessant need to approach her. I lit my candle, said a brief prayer as I always did, and waited. I didn't want to interrupt her prayer.

She slowly lifted her head, and she said, without even turning to look at me, "Emily, I'm sorry. I didn't know."

Submerged

Without a second to think about it, I knew instantly who it was. *But how?* My body immediately seized, and I couldn't move. My mouth became dry, and my world started spinning.

"You're supposed to be dead. How are you here, why are you here? Are you real?"

No! I am losing my mind; I knew I would go crazy like my mom. I have lost it. I have gone mad. God, please take me now.

"I didn't die. I was saved. I was given a second chance. A chance to mourn for you. A chance to tell you I am so sorry. This was not the plan. I stand in solidarity with you, Emily. For Lulu. I wronged you. I slept with Steven; I loved Steven. I was jealous of you. You gave him what I couldn't. A beautiful little girl. Lulu."

"STOP! You're not real. Steven killed you. I heard the code blue. I was there. That was the one thing he did for me. He killed you! Six years I watched as you and he had an affair. You slept in his bed, in my home. You spent time with my daughter. You stand here and say you stand in solidarity with me? How? For years you were against me. Do you know the day before Lulu went missing Steven filed for divorce. He was leaving me for you. I can never get him back. Even now. Even after knowing his love for, you."

I dropped to my knees. I felt so confused, so broken. *What was happening to me? She couldn't be real.*

189

Submerged

She dropped on the floor with me, and she wrapped her arms around me. She held me until I calmed myself. She whispered in my ear, "you may not believe me now, but I am here for you. Follow through with the plan. For yourself and for Lulu," I felt her release, and I opened my eyes to see Charlie standing above me.

"Charlie, what's happening? Where is Monica?"

"Monica? I didn't see anyone, Ms. Emily. Are you okay?"

"No. I'm not okay. Please take me home. I need to rest."

Upon arriving at home, I entered, and saw Steven in the doorway. His accusatory glare pierced through me. I wanted to reach out to him. To embrace him. To tell him what I was experiencing. I couldn't. I wanted him, I missed him. Who Was I to reach out first? My love never ended. His love ended six years ago. I looked at him in his eyes and walked right past him. No words were spoken. I wanted him to come to me. He didn't. I loved him so much. I missed him. I missed us. He would never love me as I wanted, so I chose to remember as it was and continue with the plan.

Monica was with me daily. I saw her everywhere. It ended up becoming a normal part of my day. Talking with her, plotting together. She hated him just as much as I did. I hated her, but I couldn't get rid of her. She followed me everywhere. It didn't take long for me to realize I had lost my mind, but at this point I couldn't resist it. It made it easier for me to follow through. The only time I could escape her voice in my ear was after my meetings when I would have a cocktail and Charlie would take me for a drive. The alcohol numbed the sound of her. This made it more difficult to remain sober. I had to be strong. I had to continue this façade just a bit longer until I knew it was time.

****

Nights were the worst. I had a tough time sleeping. My thoughts were racing, and I constantly felt like the devil was knocking on my door. My dreams took me to places I didn't want to be. Dreams of drowning in a frozen lake where Lulu took her last breaths to watching Steven fucking Monica. A montage of images that haunted me nightly. Long gone were the dreams of a happy ending. This morning, I woke up with a gut wrenching feeling of loss and betrayal. I couldn't stand to go through this anymore. Going through the motions of our false marriage. The empty feeling, and fake smiles. The secret drunk road trips after AA meetings. It had to be today. Spring is here. The sun is beaming through the open windows. The translucent curtains swaying from the billowy breeze. I could hear the mourning doves and their sorrowful coos, a sign that this must end. I sat upright in the bed, glancing into the mirror. I saw Monica.

"Today is the day."

I nodded and smiled. "Indeed."

The plan came to me as the day progressed. It was not premeditated in the sense that I didn't know what was going to occur or if my plan would be fully executed. I just knew what the depths of my belly and the voices in my head were telling me.

191

Submerged

I retrieved the music box, oleander petals, and whiskey from my secret cubby and took them down to the kitchen while I fixed myself a cup of coffee. I stared at the items as my coffee brewed. I hadn't yet opened the music box. I did so now. It was magnificent. Lulu would have adored it. I then moved the items to one of our cabinets where I could retrieve them later. I rummaged through the refrigerator and pantry looking for dinner ideas. Steven loved prime rib and a good salad. That would be perfect for this glorious day. I would also make au Gratin potatoes. I put together the list of items I would need and headed to speak with Steven before leaving.

Before entering his office, I had to stop and compose myself. I had to look forgiving, eager, loving. I needed to put on a show to convince him to have dinner with me. We barely spoke to one another, and I had to be careful as to the approach. I couldn't come off as being fake. With one final deep breath, I gently tapped on his door and entered. He looked up at me surprised. He looked excited to see me, and quicky rose from his chair. His eyes looked sad, yet hopeful. He walked around the desk to come closer but stopped. It felt like he wanted to grab me and hold me. This took me off guard.

"Hi. I thought I would make you dinner. I miss our conversations and I miss being with you. Would you have time to spend with me this evening?"

I almost started to cry. Deep down I really did miss my Steven. We had so much love for one another once. I missed nuzzling my face into his neck at night and smelling him. I missed our laughter together, and I missed always communicating with one another. Once upon a time we were perfect. Until we weren't.

I was so caught up in my emotions that I even told him I loved him.

He was all too eager to have dinner and I saw him smile. The genuine smile I remembered from years ago. With his answer I backed out of the room and asked Charlie to take me to the market.

The day was moving in slow motion, but every act was effortless and felt right. I even bought a bouquet of deep violet peonies which I placed within a crystal vase that Steven and I had gotten as a wedding gift. The vase was placed in the center of the table.

I prepped the meal, leaving the salad dressing for last. I made a garlic and herb vinaigrette. A base of olive oil and red wine vinegar with the addition of honey, Dijon mustard and various herbs. Including my own special herb. Dried, muddled oleander petals. I grabbed the oleander petals from the silk sack. As I muddled the petals the aroma of sweet apricots consumed my senses. The smell was quite tantalizing, and I had imagined it would add a bit of sweetness to the dressing hoping it didn't leave a trace of anything bitter or abnormal tasting. It looked delicious.

Once everything was prepared and baking, I went off to shower and put on the sexiest dress I could find. I wanted Steven to really see me tonight. I wanted him to remember what we had and to feel like we were on the edge of perfection once more before he took his last breath. I wanted to give him everything tonight and take it away just as he did to me for all those years.

The sun was setting, and I set the table with beautiful China. I added candles and dimmed the lights. The rays of the sunset showered through the windows. I always loved the natural light that seeped in. It brought comfort.

Just as I was fixing Steven's plate he entered.

"Hi. Sit down, let me bring you your plate."

I watched as he took his place at the table. He looked young and I was attracted to him. Like a model out of *GQ* magazine. His body was cut just right, and his shirt lay perfectly. He looked refreshed. Not tired. He looked like my Steven.

I carefully adorned his plate with the food I had prepared and laced his salad with an extra dash of the dressing. Even adding a bit to his prime rib. I lay the plate before him, and he wrapped his arms around me and pulled me into him. His face buried in my stomach. He began to sob and ask me for forgiveness. He looked up. His green eyes piercing my soul.

"I forgive you Steven."

In that moment I went to retrieve the plate. I felt like I was in a trance and his words released me. I waivered for briefly in my plan.

Submerged

What the fuck was I doing? I want him. I love him. I have always loved him.

I could see Monica standing behind Steven. *"No, you don't. He hurt you. He lied and deceived you. His lies took Lulu away from you. You can't forgive him, you must continue."*

There was a war going on in my head. At the same time, I knelt on the floor, so I was looking at Steven. I put my hand on his face and told him I loved him. I started to cry as well. I too, apologized profusely and our passion for one another erupted and I found myself kissing him. We hugged and he held me. We slowly released from one another's embrace, and he looked at me and said, "We are going to be okay."

I got up and said, "Yes. Yes, we will be okay." I turned and sat down.

"Let's eat before the food gets cold."

I knew I only had a small window of time left with him. The sun was now set, and the room was dark, except for the flames from the candles and the dimmed overhead lights that illuminated and set the tone.

This was going to go one of two ways. Either Steven would die or just get a severe case of food poisoning. Either outcome was okay with me. I will let the roulette of fait step in.

Submerged

The food smelled exceptional and tasted divine. I didn't realize how hungry I was. It had been a while since I prepared a meal. We ate in silence. Occasionally glancing up at one another. Steven even commented on the food stating it was the best he had in a while. I noticed he had a white envelope lying next to him on the table. It was addressed to me. Before I could inquire about it, Steven began coughing and he was sweating a bit. Nothing too alarming. It was as if he had a piece of food that went down the wrong pipe.

"Are you ok? Do you want water?" He nodded.

I stood and headed to the kitchen. I took down two glasses. One I filled with water, the other my top shelf whiskey. Carrying both to the table I sat next to him, handing him the water. His demeanor was distraught, and he couldn't speak. He had a difficult time sipping his water and his face was turning red. I could see he was looking at my glass. He wanted to say something. The words just couldn't come out. As I watched I sipped my drink and felt the smooth whiskey coat my throat and slide into my belly making it warm. I closed my eyes briefly to enjoy the taste, to enjoy this moment. Opening them I could see he was reaching for me. I leaned back and he fell off the chair grabbing his chest. I stood, with my glass in hand. I stood over him for a moment.

Monica was standing next to me.

"I'm so proud of you, Emily."

Submerged

I considered calling 9-1-1. I could've saved him, but I didn't want to save him. I was surprised that I had no emotion. I had no reflex to approach him or attempt to save his life. This was a sign to let it be.

I went into the kitchen, grabbed the music box and walked up the stairs to Lulu's room. I had not entered her room since she left us. It was still as she left it that morning. Clothes were lying on the floor. Her hairbrush and hair accessories laid out on her vanity. I picked up her brush and plucked a piece of her hair. She was still here. I picked up her pillow and pressed it against my face, inhaling her scent. It was too much. I began to cry. Every memory of her, every one of her laughs, every one of her tears, came flashing before me. There I stood numb. I turned on the carousel light and watched as it rotated and projected colorful silhouettes of the animals on the walls and ceiling. I remembered how fascinated Lulu was with it and how she couldn't go to sleep unless her special light was on. I wound up the music box. I took one more sip of my whiskey and laid on her bed staring up at the ceiling listening to Frere Jacques. I lay there waiting until it was over.

Submerged

Chapter 12
Letter from David

Submerged

Emily,

You don't know me, but you need to know the truth about what happened to your daughter.

I did not mean for your daughter to die. It was an accident. I'm sure Monica has given you some dirty version of what transpired but I can assure you she was the mastermind behind the kidnapping. It was her plan to hurt him and you. I'm a swindler and thief. Not a murderer. The plan was to return Lulu to you unharmed. On the day of the kidnapping, I met Monica at the movie theatre. I waited by the door. It was packed. The line to the concession stand was near the door, so it was easy to be out of sight of the cameras and to conceal what we were doing. I approached Lulu from behind with a cloth of chloroform. I gently covered her mouth and she fell into me. I picked her up and carried her to my car. I placed her in the back seat. That day, it was snowing heavily, and the snow had turned to sleet. The plan was to take her to a designated area on the outskirts of town and keep her there until the ransom was picked up. As I was driving, Lulu woke up and she was scared. She started screaming. A deer ran out in front of me. I panicked and swerved off the road into a frozen embankment. I hit my head hard and it knocked the wind out of me. When I came to and looked in the back seat, the back door had been open, and I could see your daughter running towards the frozen lake. I exited the car and ran towards her. In one quick instant I heard the lake cracking and then she was gone. I tried to go out onto the lake to help but as I wandered out it started to crack even more. I left the scene. I left your daughter in the frozen waters to die. For this I'm sorry. I cannot live with this anymore. I have so much guilt from what happened. I know someone has been following me. I'm sure that your husband has had people looking for me, but I couldn't bear to let them kill me, so I am doing it myself. Consider this my gift to you. I pray that you can forgive me and that this letter will bring you closure.

-David

Submerged

Acknowledgments

First, I thank God for giving me the gift of creativity. I thank my husband and three children, Lee, Sophia, Isabella, and Lena. You have supported me on my journey to make my dreams come true. Each of you has cheered me on and reminded me every single day that I could do this. I have my own cheerleading squad!

Thank you to my wonderful review team. Melanie, Michele, Adam, Josh, and Tae. You all took time out of your own day-to-day activities to read my work and give me the honesty I asked for. Not only are you dear friends but I value your opinions and the constructive criticism.

Thank you to my mom, Michele, my brother, Carl for always believing in me.

Lastly, I thank my dad. I know you are in heaven smiling down on me. Thank you for always letting me know how special and talented I was even when I didn't believe in myself. You always encouraged me to keep going and it's your voice I hear when I need that continued encouragement.

Much love,

Chloe

Submerged

204

Made in United States
Orlando, FL
02 October 2024

52232933R00114